DREAM

A COSMIC THRILLER OF LOVECRAFTIAN HORROR

DANIEL WILLCOCKS

DEVIL'S ROCK
PUBLISHING

OTHER TITLES BY DANIEL WILLCOCKS

Novels

When Winter Comes

The Rot Series (with Luke Kondor)

They Rot (Book 1)

They Remain (Book 2)

Keep My Bones

Anthologies

Twisted: A Collection of Dark Tales

The Omens Call

The Other Side

Other Works

The Nest

Keep up-to-date at

www.danielwillcocks.com

Ebook ISBN: 978-1-914021-22-0
Paperback ISBN: 978-1-914021-23-7
Cover art by CreativeParamita
www.devilsrockpublishing.com

For Bailey.
My favourite wonder of this cosmos.

Imagination is the only weapon in the war against reality.

— LEWIS CARROLL

We live on a placid island of ignorance in the midst of black seas of infinity, and it was not meant that we should voyage far.

— H.P. LOVECRAFT

CONTENTS

CHAPTER 1
DOWN THE RABBIT HOLE

enry's dreaming again. Caught in the clutches of his fever, his trembling lips whisper silent stories.

They tell a tale that I've never heard before, but which feels primordially familiar. Out of the pair of us, it's Henry that must suffer. Henry who must lie awake nights with needles and hornets swarming through his body, never giving him a moment's peace. Henry who tosses and turns, sweating out this unfair sickness as I mop his brow and pick at the cuticles from my worrying fingers. Henry who shoulders the evils of the world so that I may laugh and play and love when the sun is up and the world is green and Mother's home and dotes on my baby brother's every scream and utterance.

We are far too young for this.

I am far too young for this.

I paw at aching eyes. Glance at the flickering light of the oil lamp, its flames casting illusions of monsters and fairy-tale things against the wall. At night the shadows come alive, play tricks with my sleep deprived mind, and it's all I can do to tell myself the words that Father has shared with me so many times before putting horse to trap and setting out into the wild unknowns.

"There are no such things as monsters."

I scoff. Drag a hand through bedraggled, blonde hair. Wipe the greasy residue on my white pinafore. The sleeves of my azure dress have turned shades of midnight ocean in the gloom of the chamber. I can smell Henry's sickness in the air, a salt tang that speaks of tossing waves and breaking surfs of void-wrath black. My gorge rises and, for a moment, it's all I can do not to hurl into the rusted bedside bucket as another fresh torrent of abuse conquers my darling brother's insides.

"... no... please... down the... he... he can't... she... she won't..."

I cock my head, virgin brow creasing with concern. His eyelids flicker, legs thrashing at the thin, soiled sheets which peel like dampened paper beneath his chitinous frame.

"... leave her... not... not yours..."

I lean closer, cloth in hand. Prepared and dutiful to the dewy worry on his brow as his words shift to ramblings. As eyes snap open with fear, pupils roll to backs of sockets, and alarm shocks his nervous system.

"Ph'nglui mglw'nafh... Ph'nglui mglw'nafh... Cthulhu... *Cthulhu!*" A sudden intake of air as if wheezed through pipe. Eyes fixed to mine. Oh, so white and wide. Words like crumbling dust. *"Ph'nglui mglw'nafh Cthulhu R'lyeh wgah'-nagl fhtagn!"*

And now he is choking, body smashing repeatedly against his bedclothes. Limbs flailing like marine creatures of no bone structure. Mouth caught in a permanent O of pain as the sheets slip and threaten to expose my naked brother to the open air. With instinct and reflex instilled by Mother, I mount Henry and bear my full weight on his shoulders. Still him in place. Wrangle the virgin bronco as he protests with strength that should not be his after so much time spent ill, neck straining, muscles knotted, teeth clamped and bared as Henry's strange mutterings persist and leak through ivory gaps with a gentle whistle.

"It's okay... It's okay... Alice is here... You're going to be okay," I stutter through tear-blurred eyes. As I hold him, I close my lids and dream that I'm far away from this place, relief softening my pre-pubescent shoulders as I picture far-off shores, vibrant flamingos, blood-red roses in a court of candy hearts. "You're safe. Soon you'll wake up and this will all be over. It's all just a dream—"

"*Alice!*"

Blinding white lights explode in my vision as my stomach topsy-turns and the air flees my lungs. Hot, burning pain spikes my coccyx and I'm tossed against the wall, the shape of his foot already reddening my porcelain skin. I hit the wood with a crash and a feeble cry escapes my lips. Hot waves rush to my eyes, but before I can feel any pity or anger I find myself staring up at the frail young skeleton that dominates my view. A skeleton that had once been my brother.

He stands at the end of his bed, sheets slipped from his pathetic frame, nothing to leave to the imagination. What had once been a plump stomach and developing shoulders are now wet rags hanging over a scarecrow's structure. A thatch of unkempt hair—patches damp, patches straw dry —stick out in all directions, and the ghosts of Christmas' past, present, and future linger in the haunting bags beneath his eyes.

Lightning tears the darkness, turns soft edges into polygon corners. In the fraction of a second in which the world is washed with white I'm certain that I see something dark and long and sentient crawl back inside the cavern of his gaping mouth.

I take a rattling inhale. "Henry?" Words fall like empty promises.

There's no reply in voice, only a shaking hand fighting gravity as Henry's tight fist unfurls a single, reluctant finger toward the glass panes behind me. I become instantly aware of an odious ticking, yet it's only as I turn to see what it is that Henry is indicating that I realise it's not ticking at all, but the beat-drum syncopation of rain upon the glass.

When did it start raining? When did the nights fall so dark?

I return my gaze to Henry, curiosity fighting with exhaustion as I discover that Henry is not only no longer standing at the end of the bed, but that he never was at all. From my vantage on the floor, I can only make out the soft slopes of his sheets against his body. Restful and subdued in the wake of his latest fit. His gentle snores filling the room.

I rise and return to his bedside. Place a clammy palm upon a clammy brow. He is lost again, faded into his world of dreams as a gentle smile pulls at his lips.

I swallow dryly. Scratch my chin. Sip the last dregs of water from his cup. On his bedside sits a storybook, thick and worn. Pages dog-eared and stained with time. On its cover, embossed in a rust that might once have been gold, a creature of ungodly proportions disguised as a fable for children. All dragon wings and impossibilities.

I stroke a gently finger across the leather. Feel the skin of its cover pucker and kiss my touch. I draw back, a flash of Henry's skeletal ghost filling my eyelids.

Henry *had* been awake, hadn't he? I'd seen him, standing there. My back, still hot from the impact of my fall, throbs and tells me true. He *had* been awake.

Then how is he so lost in his sleep, right now? How had such movement come from a boy who had barely lifted his head in days?

Perhaps I should be sleeping, too. After all, Mother cautioned me of my unauthorised, late-night visits. Had found me slumped over his bedside most mornings. Told me that insomnia, exhaustion, and anxiety were an awful recipe for a growing, fertile mind. Could break reality and bring monsters through dimensions.

"There are no such things as monsters."

I rise, phantom-like, to my feet. Stroke Henry's head and plant a soft kiss on his temple. Feel the butterfly kiss of blood beneath the film of his skin. I stray to the window, staring into the blackness of the storm and watch the rain for what feels like hours, feels like seconds, could be never. I glimpse the shadow of the dilapidated barn at the end of the garden, horses and oxen stabled inside. Beyond that, a forest of oaks. Resources for firewood and timber, grown from eons of our own forebears. Father once proudly kept his estate, but since Henry's affliction he had fallen ever more distracted. Absent. Failure carved in the arid desolation of his own face.

There was only so much hope that prayers and well wishes could deliver to a dying world.

Another wash of lightning.

A flash of white.

It can't be...

I cup my hands, press my forehead against the cool glass. Wrestle with reality.

Blink.

Wait.

Watch.

The night falls dark.

I dare not move. I know what I have seen, yet I know it cannot be so. To acknowledge what my eyes are telling me they see could break—*would* break—me. Shatter worlds and plunge me into insanity. A place Father has sworn there is no return.

Behind me, Henry has fallen silent. I turn. He is no longer there. Just crumpled sheets and sweat-soaked pillows.

My heart is a moth trapped in a glass. *Where is my brother?*

Another flash and my fragmented thoughts confirm the impossible. He's still down there, rain-soaked and frantic. A young boy, naked and bone china white. Something bright flickers in his vapid gaze and it's in this moment that caution is discarded and I tear from Henry's bedroom. Soft feet pad across the landing, elbow crook catching the handrail and pivoting me down the stairs. I take them two at a time, almost three. Stumble, pinwheel, recover. Another flash of lightning limns the house with ghosts and the creatures from beneath my bed, shadows racing across the walls to catch me as I flee toward the absurdist creation the night has conjured, already certain that as I break into the night and feel the healing properties of Mother Nature's rain on my face that what I know to be false will be proven rightly so.

But it's not.

He's truly there. Waiting at the end of the pebble-dashed drive, Henry stands, a twisted creation of his own feverish dreams. It's Henry, but not Henry, as though a child has moulded the clay into an absurdist creation. Both a rabbit and a boy is all I can think to compare. Henry's height, but with a crook in his back and feet that appear too large for his frame. Where bare flesh should cover his bones are instead tufts of ragged white fur, sodden and glued to his skin. Long ears sit atop his head that traipse to his hind quarters. Chest rising and falling in rapid flutters as eyes as black and gleaming as pool balls stare at me in terror.

Eyes that don't register familiarity with their own sister.

"Henry?" Soft. Stolen by the wind and the howling rain. I paw drops from my eyes, shield myself from its assault with a forearm. Take a step toward the creature.

He hops back, a long, single bound. Breaks eye contact and looks skittishly around. I wonder if the poor beast is frightened. If this brother-leporine creation is true, or if I am not dreaming. Where it might have come from. How such a magnificent and tortured creation could find itself in my own back garden rather than tucked safely in bed or nested in a hole in the ground.

"Henry?" I try again. Extend a hand. Swallow rainwater. Shiver.

The Henry-rabbit looks up at the house. At his bedroom. As I follow his gaze another flash of lightning illuminates the house in ghoulish palettes, the architecture grinning like some sentient giant. At its far reaches its monstrous eye winks, and in the place where its pupil should be I find the shadow of my true brother at the window, beaming down at us both, beating at the glass until red appears from the ring of his fists and stains the window pink.

"Henry!" I call, only to be drowned out by thunder. By the time I remember the Henry-rabbit, I turn to find that that he is no longer standing, but sprinting away from the house and toward the forest.

A longing glance back. Brother-mine is gone. Never was. Could never have been.

And then I'm running. Tearing across the lawn as grass and mud French-kiss the soles of my bare feet. Wind whips at my clothes, forces me back like a physical thing but I find something hidden deep inside that pulls me towards this twisted creation. A voice, desperate and crying in the back of my skull spurs me onward, and it's all I can do to obey its command and pursue this hybrid impossibility.

Beneath my feet, turf turns to mud turns to sticks and detritus. The rain eases a fraction as I enter the womb of the woods, darting between trees, leaping over roots, batting at branches. A thousand paper cuts slice my bare arms as twig-like fingers snatch at me, the trees appearing to move of their own volition to bar my passage. The Henry-rabbit is no longer a constant thing, but a strobe of white that flashes and darts and somewhere in the air the crashing of thunder grows more frequent and urgent.

And suddenly I'm there. In the place where my rabbit-brother once was.

I stand alone in the hollow, a strange and eerie silence befalling the world. In this place there is no rain is no thunder is no lightning is no Henry is no pain is no suffering is no time. A buttery light illuminates the space and I have no indication of its source, only a marrow-deep understanding that this place has been built for me in this moment and I am the sole possessor of each fibre of this story.

I smile. Breathe deep of the honey-scented foliage. Shake off the remaining drips of a rainstorm that never was and never would be again. Spot the tuft of white fur caught on the frayed edges of the knotted hollow of an ancient oak. Drink in the splendour of the majestic totem. A tree larger than any before witnessed in my growing years. Wide at the base, obese and stumpy, reaching up and splitting into two fat arms that lift into the air as if frozen midway through a ritualistic, interpretive dance. Spindly, jagged fingers reaching out to throttle the sky.

Squeeze.

Squeeze.

Squeeze.

Smile.

For that was what this hollow was, wasn't it? A large, nurturing grin from a greater god. An invitation for better things to come. A place where all creatures could be safe, and where harm was a word never to exist in its lexicon.

A giggle escapes my throat, spurred by a dream-like haze as spores and fireflies circle my head. I find myself swaying as a strange melody fills the hollow, is heard inside my flesh, played on the strings of my nervous system, sending signals to the parts of my lizard brain that have laid dormant for centuries.

Old Knobbly-knee, daddy-dee, what gifts I bring for thee.

"Old Knobbly..." My words as insignificant as dew drops.

The song continues...

...the thyme of life and the buzzing of the bee...

"Yes. Yes..." Breathless. Stolen.

...make us big and wide and fat...

Eyes closed. Pained cheeks. Have I ever smiled this wide? Something coils around my ankle, wet and purposeful.

...*Old Knobbly-knee...*

I laugh. Gasp. Fall. The thing wrapped around my ankle tugs with painful certainty, sending me reeling again to my back. It's okay, though. The forest floor protects me, beds of leaves softening the blow as I glance at my captor and let out a sky-piercing scream of anguish at the blackened tendril that trails from Old Knobbly's scar-like maw like a charred, cephaloid tongue. Its hold is a vice and either the tree grows larger or I grow smaller as I am drawn inside Knobbly's hollow where I am fed to the great totem. Fingers grasp knotted edges that suddenly sharpen to files and break the skin of my fingers in their predatory teeth, and before I know what's happening I'm falling...

...falling...

...falling...

...falling...

Blackness swallows me. A darkness that could never be a colour, but could only be a living, breathing thing. There is no hole that I fell through—never was a hole—only the sensation of a world forever shifting and morphing in rapid, looping stages. Only a world with no constant and within which the only thing that could ever exist—has ever existed—was a little lost girl named Alice.

I scream with no sound. I blink with no distinction that tells me when eyes open and when they close. I fall with no end. Only in my mind's eye do I see the images. See my brother tossing in his fever. See the rain falling in sheets and the ghost of my mother's smile. Smell my father's cologne and watch as a rabbit runs in circles on the lawn, gigantic and fearsome, treading muddy trails in concentric patterns as I am hypnotised and fed into the old man in the tree.

I am dreaming.

Must be dreaming.

I am falling.

Soon I will wake.

Soon sense will restore and colour will return and I'll know that this is not death, for death is an end and in the end there is nothing—or, so I'm told. In death there is no falling. Is no screaming. Is no endless void filled with dense gravity that hurtles me into an endless chasm for eons and seconds all at once.

I cry.

Chest hitches.

Can't catch breath.

Still falling.

Still dreaming.

Screw eyes tight.

Flail arms.

Remember my brother.

Recall the softness of his sweat-soaked linens.

Open my eyes.

Instantly regret my actions.

The darkness has broken and, in its wake, monsters swim.

At first, I can't tell if there are hundreds of smaller monsters, or just one gigantic being. They manifest as a swarming mass of creation. As the thousand tentacles of a colossal squid, writhing and dancing on the edges of my field of vision. Swimming in a gelatinous miasma that sends out a putrid stink that gags and chokes. As I fall, they surround me. Never quite touching, yet somehow always watching. Eyes, so many eyes, opening and closing along tendrils the thickness of houses. Shots of bioluminescence snake along their coils in neon greens and blues and crimsons, and as I call out with no sound they communicate with their disinterest. Unblinking, staring eyes the size of swimming pools surrounded by brothers and sisters that blink and squint and watch with strange sucking and popping utterances that recall my own squirming episodes in the clutches of Grandma's kisses.

Somewhere in the midst of it all, the throbbing pound of a beating heart. Its steady rhythm enough to match the pulsations in my head, as though with each *boom-boom* it contracts and expands with the pressures of the universe. Pushing the titanic squid-like mass closer...

Closer...

Ever closer, and I think that this is now forever. This is all that was and all that will be and I am lost and alone in this writing conglomeration. Frozen in a stasis so nightmarish that escape is just a memory of hope. That all that once was—

Hot pain shoots up my spine.

A blink and they're gone, and I am landed with a thump on the cold, hard ground.

What is happening to me?

It's a question that stains my lips. Scents my tongue. As I lay on the unyielding, stony ground, frosted with moisture, I allow a moment for the pain to subside and for my world to stabilise. I feel as though I have spun in a centennial of circles, have been tossed and thrown by raging oceans. I draw in long gasps of an air that tastes like the dawning of time, and as I peel myself off the brownstone I no longer feel a young girl, rather that I have aged a century in my own body. My heart stammers, struggles to catch the breaths it lacked in my fall as I examine the long tunnels of this vast new cavern that stretches out in all directions.

What gifts I bring for thee. Old Knobbly. His voice a phantom in my head.

Or, so I believe at first...

Ph'nglui mglw'nafh Cthulhu R'lyeh wgah'nagl fhtagn.

I know those words. Whispers in my head echo a moment shared in a world just abandoned. Words wept from the tongue of a fever-stricken boy.

The chanting grows louder.

"Ph'nglui mglw'nafh Cthulhu R'lyeh wgah'nagl fhtagn."

They're nearby.

"Ph'nglui mglw'nafh Cthulhu R'lyeh wgah'nagl fhtagn!"

Voices. So many voices, trailing through the cave. A chorus of chants echoing thoughts that led me here, into the cave in which I can no longer find any discernible entrance above me, only stalactites that glint and drip like the teeth of Transylvanian Counts. I start forward, the only direction I can truly go, towards the signs of life that reach me in decibels as my gentle feet whisper across the rough, frigid rock. The way is lit with the glow of foreign fungi, round and bulbous, casting back the visage of blinking eyes in the writhing dark. They gather in clumps, a soft haze of spores surrounding their luminescence, the bulbs swelling and contracting as though scenting their visitor, beating like a cold, dying heart.

The chants raise in volume. "Ph'nglui mglw'nafh Cthulhu R'lyeh wgah'nagl fhtagn."

It is melodic. Ghoulishly beautiful. My skin turns to gooseflesh and I am thrown back to Sundays at church as monotony accompanies melody and the dozens of alls become a single one in the gloom. A single voice spreading the gospel of the Lord, relaying love and hope and honour and valour and sacrifice.

"Ph'nglui mglw'nafh Cthulhu R'lyeh wgah'nagl fhtagn!"

Feverish. Desperate.

Glorious.

The cave's throat widens, opens into a yawning mouth. There is water, bracken and prehistoric in its scent, awakening nerves and cells that have remained stagnant for eons inside my body. The chanters stand before the shore of the vast underground lake, cloaked and hooded in black, dozens of them in a huddle that shivers and vibrates with its keenness. I see no faces among them, only their humanoid form garbed in robes that sweep the cavern floor, an emblem of crimson hearts stitched onto their backs, visible in the glow of the spectral blue torches they carry. Where aortic valves should sit on the illustration are instead more tentacles and appendages, and I begin to wonder what it is I have wandered into.

This land of wonder.

I watch them for a short spell. Let the chanting rhythms beat my heart drum. Eyes drawn to the mirror-stillness of the lake's surface. In its depths, something glows and frolics. In the distorted world beneath the water's surface something monstrous threatens to wake. I can feel it. Can smell it with each hair in my nostrils. Can taste it in the electricity in the air as the feverish chants of this strange cult grow wild.

I take a small step forward.

Stop.

Freeze.

Cock an ear. Listen out once more for the squelching

smacks of the thing that moves behind me. Something that whines in the frequencies of dog whistles and beckons my attention away from the lunatics at the water's edge.

When I do finally yield to my own fears, I wish I'd never turned around. Some things are better left unseen. Some creations should never be realised, told, or remembered. Some monsters should stay beneath the bed.

I run, choosing flight over fight. Pick a tunnel at random. Run faster than I knew I could. Legs pumping against stone, sound lost to the cultist's choir, wind whipping blonde hair behind my ears and spraying back tears which threaten to blur my vision. I zigzag in the primordial hollows of the tunnels, descend and ascend in the intestines of this great stone beast until there is no more coil left to unravel. Until I am staring at a cold, hard wall of stone and know that there is nowhere left to flee. There is only an up into a chute devoid of light and I am trapped.

The creature trail toward me, echoes magnifying its gelatinous impossibilities that suck and sip and pop. A monster without true definition, and so many mouths. My lips tremble as Henry's once did in a world that is not this one. I wonder if the nightmares of his fever match my present reality as my body racks with sobs and the tears begin to trail down my cheeks. I press to the wall, the only comfort offered to be found in its cool touch on my feverish skin as the tears begin to flood.

The tears rain down.

The tears splash the rock.

The monster approaches.

Water gathers around my toes. Around my ankles. Rises to my knees. Each tear drop magnified and grown into a dark pool that fills this cavernous space.

I gasp at the sight of the panicking creature, flailing and

terrified, unable to comprehend this turn of events. I close my eyes. Take myself far away from this place. Far away from endless falling and ancient oaks and gelatinous monsters and heaving cults...

...far away from the invasive truth that whispers in the back of my head.

The truth that I cannot swim.

And the water is rising.

CHAPTER 2
AN OCEAN DEEP

The monstrous gurgling of the thing I cannot not name resounds behind me. My hands grow slick with tears as I attempt to shut out the light and picture a place that was once happy. A place that was never this one. In my manufactured darkness I see a meadow, laced with golden flowers that rise to ankles and tickle flesh. Clouds like gossamer strewn across an azure sky. One hundred yards away, Henry laughs, skips, plays with Howard, our family beagle, dead for years but never forgotten.

Henry runs. Tosses the pig skin. Elicits Howard's yammering barks. Draws closer under the dazzling sun. Pink-cheeked and plump. I wait with hands on hips, a stark cosmic mirror of my mother from an alternate timeline. Laugh. Find myself drawn to the flowers and grasses that grow and creep up my legs. Green blades and buttery blossoms crawling around my calves like insectoid antennae, stalking up my thighs. Among the grasses I see snakes and wonder then if the gelatinous creature with its strange appendages has invaded even this private world of mine, as though this violation was just one of so many wonders of its unending possibilities.

Henry races toward me, mirth morphed to madness as his jaw drops and fear stains his eyes. The sun plummets from the sky, dragging clouds, collecting birds, taken by a distorted and sudden rush of gravity as all light fails, and even the moon hides its face this night.

It is warm around my waist, and I realise then that Henry is hugging me, arms wrapped tightly. Only, when I open my eyes, it's not Henry, and the only consolation that finds me is the reality that I haven't allowed my bladder its uncontrolled eruptions. It's the only solace that can be as I stare about the growing body of water that fills the cavern, the miasmic creature nowhere now to be seen. There is no longer an exit to this place, the walls sealed and shut, and as I hunt for the source of the water's flow, I begin to understand that the source of this rising tide is my own unhappiness and terror. I cannot prevent the tears trailing from my cheeks, and with each droplet that ripples the surface of this fetid new pond, the water swells and levies until it is to my neck and I know that soon I shall drown.

My breath comes in aching hitches. I wish I did not cry but fear has overtaken and now the dewy pearls come in rapid succession, and I am rising.

Rising.

Lifting through the chute of this strange new world as though expelled through the granite throat of a gagging stone golem. Water swirls around me and drags me beneath and I am privy to a world of liquid wonder. With each rising note, the cavern below fades from view and silver shoals glimmer around me, dart like dust in sclera, can never be captured, can never be witnessed in true. I hold my breath, lungs aching for oxygen as I both sink and rise and whorl and twist and drown and ascend and marvel at the monstrous things that I imagine in the dark. My eyes sting from sobs. My eyes sting from salt. Currents and tides form and I am thrown around green and mirky waters, buffeted by invisible tides, as aquatic life diversifies and gives me a glimpse of the evolution of the world. Crustaceans, cephalopods, all manner of bony, jawless, and cartilaginous fish flock and scurry and flee from my presence. I spy clownfish and porpoise, dance with mermaids and manatees, drown among colossal squid and leviathan...

...fight for air.

Reach an arm.

Find no purchase. No salvation.

My body judders and shakes, throat belching bubbles that obscure the view of this wonderland.

Laugh. Allow the passage of my own salty tears to race down my gullet.

Surrender.

Find peace as I float.

As I drift.

As I fall...

Fireworks blossom in the cavern of my mind as I drown and fade. A great smile appears in the dazzling lights, stretching from periphery to periphery, cat-like and serene, yet I know this must be Henry. A smile just for me. A smile to bring me peace as I gargle my final notes and accept my watery fate...

...allow myself to end...

It is so peaceful here in dying. So calm. So still. I am gently rocked in the arms of the Lord, cradled in his bosom as light grows around me and I know that I am His. I will meet the rest here soon. My family. My loved ones. I will await their ascension into Heaven. We will laugh about this fever dream of mine, and that will be the end of it. Reminisce of our mortal time on Earth and—

"Wake up!"

Hot pain flares across my cheek.

"Alice! No, no, Alice! Wake up. Please."

Another strike of the iron. Searing and whip-sharp.

"No, no, no, no." The desperate sound of a man that I once knew. A man that raised me, sat on wrinkled sheets at my bedside and coddled my ills. "This isn't funny, anymore. Please, Alice. Wake up!"

A third strike that jolts me from my wooden bed and sets me upright. My head swims as the ocean expels itself from my lungs and across my lap in a lukewarm torrent. My tonsils protest. Throat is scratched and raw. Has anyone ever vomited this much salt water?

"Oh, thank goodness." A relieved chuckle. "You're alive. Thank Azathoth, you're alive."

Azathoth?

I look up into the face of my father. No... not my father. A cruel and twisted distortion of my father staring back at me. By all accounts it is he, chestnut eyes and crooked nose —a small scar on his left cheek from tripping in the barn and catching his face on the splintered door—but it is also an alarming number of malformities that steal my inhalations. Springs to mind haunting visages of my rabbit-brother.

For my father's skin is a putrid green, slimed and scaled in mottled patches. His head is domed, hairless and gleaming under the silver glow of a sickle moon that looms threatening in the sky. Where there should have been ears are instead two small holes, and a selection of claw-like gashes pink his neck and pucker in animated, shallow gasps like the gills of a submerged creature.

I shuffle back, splinters hooking barbs on the pads of my palms as I grow the distance between us until the side of the watery vessel prevents further escape, and I see for the first time that I am on a large wooden ship. A tattered sail flaps in the breeze as white foam waves rattle around us, dizzying our motion on an endless emerald ocean. Accommodating the deck are more of the haunting green figures, less man and more fish than my father, oblivious to his current plight as they set about their duties and operate their maritime duties.

"Alice...?"

My father draws closer. I know as well as he does that there is nowhere left for me to go. My head pounds, throat itching and yet somehow impossibly dry despite the truth that only moments ago I had believed myself drowned. I stare unblinking, uncertain of my next move. Every play of intention I have taken since leaving home has only sped up this nightmarish rollercoaster, and I dare not imbalance the scales further.

"Alice." He casts a cruel illusion of a smile. Sharp, filed teeth like thumb tacks embedded in his blackened gums. "Oh, Alice. You're here. It's really you. They said that you wouldn't come, but here you are. At last. The one who will set us free."

"Father?"

My fish-father glances over his shoulders, certain that I have spotted someone to whom he is yet unacquainted.

"You," I confirm. "You are not...?"

"Your father?" My fish-father's grin widens, splitting his face horizontally in two. He arches back, rents an explosive bark to the skies as lightning crashes on the horizon and thunder drowns his haunting belch. "Oh, I'm sorry, Alice. I am not your father, no. But you are our mother, aren't you? The one who was sent to set us free. To break our chains and end this tidal pool of infinity." His eyes sparkle, hope shining like diamonds in his black pupils. "It's really you. You're here."

"I don't understand...What are you saying?" I ask, finding a courage that has lain dormant. "Who's here to save you? How do you know my name?"

He crosses the threshold between us, crouches to eye level. His shoulders are broad, blocking out my view of the ship, but not quickly enough for me to abandon the image of the giant white blubbery swell I just glimpsed breaking the waves before disappearing beneath the waters. "*You* are here to save us, Alice. It's as the prophecies have foretold. A virginal human plucked from the waves, able to tread the boundaries of reality to end Her reign of terror."

Hot tears prick my eyes, brought forth from the offence of this new scent. This fish-father creature that stinks of coastlines and seaweed, offal and ocean. A creature that brings my gorge high in my throat and threatens a fresh lashing of brackish water from the depths of my exhausted stomach.

When I reply, my voice is weak. "I don't understand..."

"It's written in the scripture!" my fish-father declares, frenzied with excitement as he paces back and forth before me, hands exploring the slick dome of his head, eyes alight like the birth of stars. "The book. It's in the book, Alice. It's written in the pages, passed down for generations. For aeons we have sailed, searching for land, never finding coastline, and yet... here you are. Birthed from the waters. Blonde-haired and blue eyed and oh so real."

I force myself to my feet, fighting shaking knees. My patience grows thin, world tossed from pillar to post in the wake of my brother's vacancy. Hot anger surges my veins and before I'm aware of what I'm doing, my fists are beating his chest. His rib cage defends his organs, shallow skin yielding beneath each pound like moist dough. The others of his kind pause and study my attack, and with one final shove of pent-up rage I force him several steps back. "Enough of your riddles. Speak clearly and true. Tell me where I am. What am I doing here? How do I free myself of this place? Where is my brother? How do I get home?"

Waves rise around us, as if emboldened by my own inner tempest. Lightning blinds in strobic bursts, breaks the sky in shades of neon green. Another swell of blubbery white creature like the white whale of Captain Ahab teases the ocean's surface, its mass the size of stadiums.

My fish-father looks about his comrades. The ship lists sharply, but they remain standing. Meanwhile I fight for balance. The air grows thicker with the acrid scent of offal and it's all I can do to hold his gaze under jellied legs.

"Alice..." He draws closer. I freeze. A hand that is webbed between fingers is placed on my shoulder as each word uttered sends a wave of nautical spray from a lipless mouth to my skin. "You are the chosen one, Alice. For thousands of years, we have waited for you to release us. To allow us the dockage on dry land where we may escape this endless chase from our ocean demons." Another swell and flash of white, unnoticed by my fish-father. "You are the true bearer of the Necronomicon. The one who will harness its pages and break us from the prison She seeks to bind us in. It is on you to find this artifact, translate its knowledge, and free our kind forever, before the Queen lays her hands on the relic."

"The Queen? What Queen?" In my mind I see a flash of hearts, stitched onto the back of black cloaks.

"The Red Queen," my fish-father crows, oblivious to the

23

increasing volume of slithering appendages that emerge from the water and grow closer to the ship. Surrounds the hull. Crowds the waves. "The one who seeks to awaken the great Cthulhu from his watery bed in R'lyeh."

"Cthulhu?" A book. Tentacles. A monster.

"An ancient cosmic being. The first to rise of the Great Old Ones. Should The Red Queen call Cthulhu from his slumber, all that we've ever known will crash around us, drowning us in the eternal void of darkness as she gains passage into the Dreamlands."

My head pounds. Heart races. A great scaly crown rises from the water, slicing the ocean in two like the segmented wings of a colossal bat. Each articulation spikes the sky, daggers and teeth from a monster hungry for the universe.

"I don't understand what any of this means. Isn't this the Dreamlands—"

Now the cries erupt. Now the fish figures panic, and in their frenzy all hell breaks loose. As the dome of a mono-lithic head follows the skyscraper spikes out of the ocean, the water pulses, propels us across the rise and fall of tsunamis. Great gusts rush around us as I race to the mast and hold on for dear life, my fish-father joined at the pillar with me, screaming against the spray and foam. "Find the Necronomicon, Alice. The pages will tell you what you must know. Your brother... Your world... There's only one way back... Let the Great Eye guide you."

The ship lists leeward, the bow rising into the sky. I scream as fish figures drop like raisins into the mouth of this titanic new monstrosity, a creature of hilarious and unholy proportions. Its eyes the size of cathedrals. Each one of its teeth a spire. Water drains and flushes and whirls into its cavernous maw, threatening to swallow us whole.

"What is that thing?" I scream, fingers white-knuckled as I hang over the void of this creature's gullet.

Before my fish-father can reply, the ship rights itself and the ocean quells. The untold god closes its monstrous maw, and we are granted a moment of respite as it digests its catch.

"Secure the rigging!" my fish-father bellows. "Batten down the hatches. Full speed ahead!"

"Land, ho!" a voice calls back, the insanity of the truth draining the colour from my fish-father's face. In the distance a coastline appears, a jagged strip of golden sand nestled beneath a scorching sun that has broken clouds and shines a thick ray of light upon this foreign haven, stark in contrast to the sooty sky above us. A jade forest lines the coast, the colour dazzling enough to prick the eyes.

"Full speed ahead" my fish-father confirms, bracing himself against the wind as the ship races across waves that stretch like continents, rising and falling across valleys and peaks as the mammoth titan gives chase, erupts with protest, and drives us onward. Its cries are bending metal, its calls are crashing comets. Each determined stroke of titanic arms are propellants that, in a cruel twist of its own irony, shoot us farther from its clutches.

White foam absorbs us, rains upward and cloaks our vision. I can't make out individual voices, but I can smell collective fear, that same scent that tells of urine-soaked sheets and sweat from adrenal glands. The ship bounces upward, rises on the currents and flies free, this crew of ours now suspended and slave to no more physical master for a blip in time until the shore stretches sandy fingers and draws us to its safety.

The ship grinds to a halt on sand. Cocks its head like a curious bird. Sun blinds us. Silence screams.

I wait for what feels like an eternity, gathering my breath in this temporary bubble of relief. It's at the first call of strange coastal birds that I open my eyes and peel myself from the mast. The ocean is calmed, and the only sign that remains from our unholy pursuer is the gentle gathering of foaming bubbles and the trailing of one long, sharp peak of the crown as it stalks toward the horizon and returns, disappointed, to its watery domain.

My skin prickles, sensitive and salt-stung. At the sound of timber crashing against wood I discover my fish-father has begun guiding his kin off the ship and onto the shore. They are as astounded and confused as I, eyes wide and marvelling as some drop to their knees, fingers threading through sand. Others kiss the coast, tongues spitting out grains. A small minority simply cry.

After a few breaths of recovery, I follow the remaining crew, awaiting my turn to disembark. At the bottom of the gangway, I step onto sand that should be scorching but is cool on the soles of my feet. I approach my grinning fish-father as he beckons with a long, hooked finger. "The prophecy is realised."

"What was that thing out there?" I ask, unable to shake the titan's image from my memory. I wonder if the aquatic monstrosity shall always live in the blinking darkness of my eyelids.

My fish-father looks out to the ocean, sunlight causing his chestnut eyes to gleam like andalusite. "A Dagon. A creature of the before, and the greatest nemeses of our people. We were cursed to sail these endless waters, never able to rest through fear of attack. I wondered for a moment if today would be the day our adventure came to an end, but alas, the scriptures speak true." He looks down at me. "You have arrived."

I nod, uncertain what to say. His conviction only has me more unsure, and as I find the question to ask, I already know what the answer is to become. "Why do you hold the face of my father?"

My fish-father thinks about this for a long moment, scours the sand at his feet for answers. Relinquishes. "This I do not know. This world works in mysterious ways, little one. You will find many more riddles and anomalies before your journey reaches its conclusion. It would do you well not to draw on sense if you are to survive these lands."

I sigh. Nod. Turn to the forest and bask momentarily in its wonder. The foliage is dense, green palms and fronds like verdant jewels, fungi and plant-life limning the scape like the afterbirth of a rainbow. Calls of fauna and insect fill the sky and though I am afraid, I am also resolved in my purpose.

"You spoke of a book. One that I must find to free myself from this reality?"

"I did."

"Where might it be?"

My fish-father's eyes narrow, staring in the direction I knew he would. "I cannot give you specific instruction, for all I know from the scripture is that you alone must find it. These are strange lands, filled with all manner of bizarre, wonderful, and deadly beings. Seek out the Necronomicon, and you shall find all that you need to accomplish your task."

"But..." I bite my lip. "I am afraid."

"It does not do to dwell on fear. For it is our own fear, not that of others, that holds us captive and shrinks our possibilities." A wet hand holds my shoulder. "Save fear for those who oppose you, Alice. Bringer of land. Breaker of worlds." He frowns, repeats once more, "Let the Great Eye guide you."

Knowing not what to reply, I stalk away from the fish figures, feet leaving gentle impressions in the sand. Soon enough I stand before the vast and lustrous wilderness, the air fragranced with a cocktail of dew drops and ripened things. For half a moment, I fancy that I spy the ghost of my rabbit-brother between the fronds. For half a moment, I believe I am brave enough to accomplish this task.

Steeling myself with a long breath, I take my first steps forward, feet breaking new ground into this wondrous forest as I heed my fish-father's advice and allow the Great Eye to spur me onwards.

CHAPTER 3
OF FUNGUS AND FLIES

And so, I walk on into a land of giants.

Giant trees, giant brush, giant fungi, giant fauna. A world believed to be extinct, but which presents itself in grandiose wonder, mocking me with its scale, terrifying in its sentient glory.

The trees are ancient things, planted at the dawn of creation with boughs as wide as city streets, gnarled and knotted as individual branches escape and fight to scratch the sky. Roots knot like fibrous cables turned to tangle weeds. Leaves sprout from trunks like natural skyscrapers, exploding into great umbrellas of mauve and crimson and verdant before gracefully sailing down to land around me, as though time works differently here and I am privy to the season's cycle, each spell-binding phase shifting in an instant.

Blades of grass stroke up to my chin, each dagger sharp and honed. A small blotch of blood stains my finger from my first experimentation into the forest and I am learned not to follow my curiosity with physical touch. Fungus unlike any that I have ever seen makes me wonder if I have joined my brother in his fever dreams and am experiencing some form of hallucinogenic episode. They are domed and glistening, mountainous like the cresting backs of whales, luminous as night sticks, sporting fronds that wave at me and coax me to them as I restrain and briskly walk past, resisting their spraying spores that stink so sickeningly sweet of cotton candy, my father's rose bed, and my mother's bosom. Each inhalation dizzies my senses as I place one foot in front of the other and walk on, afraid of what might happen were I to lose my sensibilities—if I may indeed be so bold as to assume that that was an eventually still to come, and not one to which I had already fallen prey.

Above me, great beasts stalk, too enormous for comprehension. Insectoid legs from terrifying arthropods stab the ground as translucent underbellies pass overhead, organs animated and throbbing in jellied stomachs, blurring out sunlight, starlight, moonlight. Upon my first entry into this absurd new section of experience I felt my heart might stop, that I may be struck instantly dead and become one with the forest, but already I have learned that I am as insignificant to them as may be the ant-life that swarms my feet in a meadow on an August day.

I think a lot of my brother as I walk. The real one. Not the horrid rabbit-brother creation of this realm. Wonder where he may be. On occasion I fancy I detect him ahead of me, teasing the fringes of my visions reach, yet with each concentrated stare I see only more foliage. There is no discernible path to follow, and so I realise the chances of my pursuit finishing in success are slim. Yet, what else must I do but journey onward and trust in hope? Although I had experienced absurd calamities that I never once would have felt would befall me, I have thus far survived. An impossible tumble into the gullet of Old Knobbly, a cavern of cultists, a gelatinous monstrosity, an ocean of my own creation, the finding of my fish-father, and the escape of the titanic sea creature were adventures I could never have imagined, and yet, here I am. I am survived.

A soft buzzing hums in the distance. I hunt for its source and am once again blind to my own curiosity. The ground is hard, and I find I must now pay extra attention to avoid chasms of cracks and breaks below me so as not to roll an ankle or fall prey to the hungry earth. I leap, skip, jump, treating the way ahead as a chalked-out hopscotch sketched into the playground's asphalt, and as I skirt the great boughs of a breed of tree I have never seen, the forest opens into a great hollow. Sunlight breaks the sky, warming my cheeks. The sky is a melted rainbow, mottled dashes of colour twisting and dancing as oil in the puddles of a rain-soaked London street. The colossal insectoid guardians give this place a wide berth, and as I enter into the hollow's heart, I begin to see the symmetry to the place that led me here on that dark and rainy night, many centuries ago.

Old Knobbly stands in the distance, rooted and as enormous as Everest to a fly. His great knotted eyes hunting and scanning, for what I do not know. The mouth I had tumbled inside is now a size beyond description and is twisted into a toothy grin that freezes my blood and gives me cause for alarm.

The humming is louder here.

I glance over my shoulder and find the way now barred by a tree that can only have shuffled toward me in a manner that staggers comprehension. Stretching in either direction are brother- and sister-trees that embrace each other like the fence posts of a titan's garden, and with a heavy sigh I relinquish to the forest and embrace my fate. There is no turning back.

But there is now a path.

As grasses grow taller around me and bar my view of Old Knobbly, I am both relieved and terrified. Though I am hidden from his watchful gaze I begin to wonder if the grasses are his minions, the trees his foot soldiers. Am I wandering through a conspiracy designed to end me and shut down this nightmarish dream once and for all?

And, oh, the humming.

It rages around me like some vengeful thing, growing louder and louder until all that I know is the marrow-deep vibrations of my soul that prickle my skin and leave me breathless. I feel its song in my teeth. It rattles each unsteady step, and just as I'm about to scream, the first of their order emerges before me.

It appears in a sudden flash of movement and colour, darting toward me stinger-first. A wasp, or so my naive mind forces me to believe, until I am recovered from my swift dive into the dusty earth and find more of them flocking my now-prone form, clouding the sky. This strange drove of wasps, with wings that should belong to bats, flesh not soft but crisp and overbaked, and oh so many legs for such a creature to bear. They hover in colours of rigor mortis. Float with no discernible facial features. Where there should be eyes are only more mouths, and in the gaps between mimic lips ululating tongues are short appendages that could only be described as tentacles that sniff and taste and scent the air. Leading the train of legs and limbs are grasping claws that call back memories of mantids and shrimps once witnessed in a classroom textbook, and before I have a chance to further assess their anatomy they are charging once again.

This time I scream, and I absurdly wonder if Old Knobbly can hear me. If it even matters. I race forward, zigzagging between their number, darting between clusters of grass as they drop from the sky and rain down on me, doggedly fixed in their purpose. Hungry for a morsel. Famished for a feast.

My naked feet propel me forward. The grasses have opened, creating a labyrinth of unintelligent design. I swiftly turn left as three of them tear by in a fevered pitch of vibration, yet this avoidance does not give me further courage. They are above me, some moving faster to block the path ahead. I twist right, grasping a blade of grass to assist the pivot and find my hand now blood-soaked and shredded to soft tissue. A satisfying smacking of mouths conjures from behind and a quick glance over my shoulder shows me half a dozen of these nightmares gather to the glistening crimson that stains the blade, drawn like sharks and delivered to their desire.

Ahead of me, one of the creatures awaits, stalking along the ground on its train of legs. It rears up, fills my vision. Hot tears burn my eyes and as I scream it stabs a bracken-thin leg at my torso. I twist, a slice opening along my navel, shredding cloth and pinking skin. Its satisfied shriek causes me to dizzy, causes my legs to tremble. One knee buckles. The creature's second strike sails over my head. I grab a handful of dust and hurl it at the creature, clouds of grit and soil finding a bed within its mouths. It chokes, staggers, reluctantly allows passage.

I skirt its body, assaulted with the scent of primordial woodland and forgotten things, and find myself once more lost in a labyrinth of emerald daggers. An idea strikes as I choose my pivots, my hand throbbing with pain as I paw a splatter of my blood on each blade I pass. They buzz frantically somewhere behind me, wet slurping and smacking kisses frolicking over my inner juices until their buzzing begins to rescind and I am left running blindly into a nowhere of my own creation. I afford myself another glance and can make out a few of their number hovering in the skies, fighting over an item I cannot see.

I slow.

Walk backwards.

Heel catches rock.

I tumble into a descent that wasn't reality a moment ago.

The world becomes a dizzying blur of green and brown as I roll downhill, arms pinwheeling for purchase, each knock against soil enough to force a grunt and gasp and moan. My skull smacks against something unyielding, sending flashes of white blossoms into my vision. My hand reaches for something—anything—to gain purchase and instead comes away further bloodied. The buzzing is a steady beat, soft and distant, but its diminishing brings me no peace as I trail away, gathering speed, knocked and bruised, tumbling, ever tumbling, until I'm tumbling no longer.

I cannot say for how long I lie there, face in the dirt. The forest taints my tongue and my body aches beyond comprehension. I am afraid to move, head filled with rattling bones and embering coals. In my mind's eye I see Henry at my side, hand on my shoulder, calling for our parents. I see Mother and Father's panic-stricken faces as Father lifts me, cradles me to his bosom and sets me into bed. By candlelight he reads to me. By moonlight Mother nurses me. Henry never leaves, a faithful dog by my side.

And I am home.

And I am safe.

And in this dream of mine, the world is right. The world is returned, and I am known.

"It does not do to dwell on dreams, Alice."

I raise my head to find the source of the voice, but instead find myself peering through blurred eyes at a mushroom farm drained of all colour but that of thatch and straw. They rise around me, cupped and fat and eukaryotic, the sudden wash of dreary mono enough to vacuum my breath. Attached to the umbrella of each fungus I spy cocoons, strung from neat webbing, the bodies of each like the flaking skin of a leper's back. Large and bulbous and swaying gently in a breeze I cannot feel on my broken skin.

I mask a scream. Clap a bloodied hand to my lips. Taste copper and iron.

"It would do you well to not rouse them," the voice says. "They are hungry when they awake. It's in their code. *Fly and feast, feast and fly, all great creatures serve the Eye.*"

I deftly ease myself from the ground, hunting for the talking creature, and find what I'm looking for a short distance above, its bulbous weight causing the cap of the fungus to droop toward me as though presenting itself in a mournful bow to a powerful queen.

"You are lost."

The creature states it not as a question, and its surety heats my insides. My lips flap like a starved fish, struggling to find words when faced with such absurdity. I fear that I may at last be going mad, knowing somewhere deep in my heart of hearts that swollen, segmented nymphs should not be capable of speech. Knowing that this bloated wasp larva should have neither tongue nor eye nor mouth nor intelligence to look down upon me and cast its judgement. Should not be wearing the face of my lost dog, Howard, canine-like but set into an insect's body. Floppy ears and a protruding muzzle. Keen eyes and a hanging tongue. Gentle reams of smoke rise around it, casting the creature in a foggy haze, and it is only then that I see that a gentle flame burns around its hefty rear, as though this monstrosity is made of paper and is gently crisping into its final stages of destruction.

"I know what it is that you seek," the nymph that is not Howard says. "For it is the very thing that all creatures of this land seek to claim. A key, if you will, into another way of being."

"What are you?"

"Mad, Alice." The creature doesn't blink. It leers down at me with a curiosity that I return, and I am hardly aware of the countless brother and sister cocoons that sway rhythmically around us.

I look down at my feet, caked in dust and dirt and dried blood. One toenail hangs on by a strand. Flesh hangs off my hands and arms like ribbons, yet no pain raises alarm. "I want to go home."

"Where is home?"

I consider his question. Realise I cannot answer it. Stay mute.

The grotesque canine-larva shifts, twisting its ember-laced stomach to the sky. The flames eat away at its paunch, a dance of concentric circles slowly working to its edges. I smell charred popcorn and melted bon-bons. "Home is relative," the canine-larva says. "For some, home is the stead in which they are born. For others, they know the truth of the cosmos. That home is the stardust in us all. An existent remained for millennia. Life has no roof, only vacuous space in which you float away your troubles into nebulae and galaxies."

"That sounds so big."

"It is big," the canine-larva agrees. "And, yet, isn't it also the smallest truth known to all that have gained sentience?" It sighs, grimaces against the burning flames that swell and spread across its papery flesh. "Wonderland is a bottle, Alice. A glass cage in which all things inside must dwell. And so, those whom are trapped inside, long for an escape. Our contents poured into the limitless pool. There is one key to unlock this door, and it would serve you well to find it, before others realise their own success."

"The book," I breathe.

The canine-larva nods, the folds of its neck attempting to constrict its movement. I search the hundreds upon thousands of suspended cocoons, see the forms of more of these creatures inside, brains moulding into a hive-like intelligence that might also be seeking the pages of this fabled tome. Wonder where to tread to hone my compass and find the thing I am bound to seek.

"It is buried," the canine-larva says, once more reading thoughts before they metamorphose to words. "The dawn of life begins with the dusk of death. The Necronomicon lies lost in a home of rattling bones and screaming souls." It points with its gaze toward a path I did not see. "Find the book, Alice. Find it before She lays claim. There are worse things in life than death. In the blurring of the two worlds, armed by its pages, She may claim dominion. That is a fate that even the great Eye does not wish to endure."

"I have heard tell of this great Eye," I reply. "I have seen its reverence beheld in the creatures of your world. Can you tell me what it is?"

The canine-larva smiles a crooked smile, revealing stringing gums devoid of teeth. "Your time grows short, Alice. Bringer of Ends."

I hear the gush of flapping wings, great sails beaten against an endless sky, and I look to the cocoons for answers. They are still, now. Frozen in a timeless tableau.

The canine-larva lets out a throttled cackle, and as I look to him I see the sky darken above, a cloud of colossal birds beating wings against the gusty currents. Dread drains what little colour remains in my cheeks, and as I set my feet to running, I can already tell that something is wrong. I am an insignificant feast-turned-hunt for these new birds that flock and swarm toward me, down into these fungal fields.

Before I get far at all, the first of their number crashes into the mushroom forest, snaps the neck of several cups of mushroom as it tumbles with a greedy satisfaction onto the dirt. Another crashes to land, bringing to my imagination the great meteors that reset the world an age before. Only, instead of rock and geology I find creatures of membrane and midnight black that stretch great wings. Unlike the waspish beings encountered in this nightmarish place, their faces are bare and plain, just a stretch of void-like skin that claims the dome of their heads. As the first of their landed number unfurls, I see a bipedal monstrosity with human-like arms and legs capped with serrated claws. A long tail whips behind the creature, and it is then that the fearful tales of my father are realised and turned true.

Early to bed, wake with the dew.
Else the fearful Nightgaunts will come for you.

It is them. The Nightgaunts. Fabled creatures of folklore and legend, turned reality. I can hardly blink or focus, only shudder and shake as I recall sleepless nights, tossing and turning in the dark, seeing their shape in the shadows of my bedroom. A harmless tale, or so my father must have believed, but one that exacted the opposite reaction to its desired effect. I had seen them before, through the eyes of a more juvenile mind, and though I had screamed and cried and demanded my father leave me a light source to sleep by, they had never truly retreated from my infantile imaginings.

For here they were. Birthed from my nightmares. This I knew with a sudden, alarming clarity. Kept alive and fuelled by the twisted worries and concerns of my darkest fears.

At first, they seem unconcerned with the frail little girl forcing slow steps to retreat from their number. Their focus honed on the breaking and destruction of the many cocoons as powerful claws tear shells and free half-formed wasp-things from their bindings. Wet strings and strange plasma slime the twisted malformations as they hit the ground with a moist smack and the Nightgaunts flock the carcasses to devour and feed. There is no screech of declaration from the Gaunts, no satisfied cry or call. They are deathly still and silent, and as I pray and wish to be anywhere but here, scream noiseless pleas for my limbs to play servant to my whims and wills, I watch in horror as three Gaunts coordinate to claim my flaming canine-larva guide. Grasping appendages that stretch like taffy in each hand, they beat their massive wings and carry the larva into the sky. Higher, ever higher they rise, the canine-larva on a bungee cord of its own organs, climbing skyward, expressionless and sending reams of smoke around this twisted image.

When it seems that they can fly no higher, they communicate without word and simultaneously release their grip on their baggage. The canine-larva gathers speed, its great body whistling towards the ground, the flames erupted and devouring the fuel of oxygen. Its eyes are closed, a serene grace that tells me that this was always written in the stars, that all moments would have led to this, and it is only when its body crashes into the ground, finds a landing place among the waiting, feasting Gaunts, that the world erupts and changes, and I am turned to flee.

Flames blossom. Spawn from the destructed body of the nymph and pulse from the source in perfect circles of pain and flames. The surrounding fungus falls first, fire latching onto their stalks, igniting the remaining cocoons. Heat throbs towards me, the Nightgaunts seemingly unaffected as they launch themselves skyward and gaze down upon the harvest fields with vapid, expressionless stares. They warble in the flames as the conflagration grows. Black plumes of thick smoke funnel into the sky, taint the air, cover me with soot and choke my throat, and I am running, running, fleeing into an unknown place where the path may lead. I turn full attention to my plight and beat feet against a ground that bites and scratches my soles, blink against stinging heat as ash swarms me, wonder where all of this might lead and where it is that I am yet to go. See my true brother's face in the smoke. See it coalesce and dissolve, coalesce and swim. See it in the foreground and all that is the horizon as the crackle of the pyre eats at shroom forest and the Nightgaunts recover from their extinction event, flame-tipped wings illuminated like necrotic fireflies that spot their prey and hurry to dine.

I navigate the stalks of flaming fungi, skin slick with sweat, using what remains of their umbrellas as cover. It is only when I can run no longer from my silent predators that I clutch a hand to my chest and the tears begin to flow. Sobs rack my stomach, and as warm tears hiss against the heated ground I wonder if escape lies once more in these salty droplets. I watch them fertilise the forest floor. Dry, cracked earth drinking hungrily and leaving only dust and the ghost of a patch behind. I can no longer see the Gaunts, but I can feel their presence, and as darkness closes in, I realise that this is not darkness at all, but their collective mass hovering around me, doming me in as the flames continue to feast and I am herded.

My stomach rumbles at the smell of the world. Sweet like honeysuckle, salted like roasted pork. My mouth involuntarily fills with saliva and before I know what it is my body does, I dig in my nails and pluck a portion of the fungal canopy above. As the oppressive ghoulish huddle closes in, I mash raw mushroom between my teeth. Before they land silently on the ground, stalking ever closer, long tails swishing and aggravating flame, I have swallowed my morsel.

And, in an instant, all the world changes.

CHAPTER 4
A BLINK OF MADNESS

Dark wings bristle and flap as sails in a hurricane. Smoke envelopes the world and cyclones in twisters around my body. Through the haze I see their silhouettes, shrinking and ever distant as my organs expand and flip and I am changed. As the smoke thins and they return to full view, I am witness to a world as glimpsed through the wrong side of the looking glass, infinitesimal and cast in miniature.

I stand swaying above the fungal field, towering my former terrorisers, the great conflagration only an ember against my toes. The Gaunts evacuate, their plight diminished as they scatter from this giant and hunt for easier prey. My new stature provides me perspective, a way to see the ancient and twisted forest that surrounds me as though I am placed in a cornfield, my head almost brushing the tops of the canopies. Colourful and fancy birds take wing, mammals scatter at my new gigantism, and yet it is only a momentary reprieve, a small glimmer of sanity amongst madness before reality finally breaks and I am returned into a state of unknown.

It begins with a step. A small feat that I had once mastered when I was no more than a babe, perfected in growing years and taken for granted. My bowels roars as I digest the mushroom, and rather than finding solid ground beneath that step, I find liquid gold that submerges toes and claims heels and instead I tumble, fall, rotate, slip into the melted works of watercolours, fungi, and rainbows. Slip into oils and a weightless world. Cross into the upside-down and free float among the neon trees that wave and bristle and undulate like pondweed. I am free. Free to drift and free to glide. An addict's smile stains chapped lips, pupils claiming dominion of sclera as I soak it all in, hallucinate, play witness to a world never before witnessed by human blood as creatures of myth and imagination dart and play and frolic and dine and copulate in the cracks between worlds. As I float away from the fast-shrinking field below the antelope graze and migrate, composed of deep aquatic blues and with more legs than must serve function. Tubular horns bedeck their flanks, and they munch with multiple heads armed with long, invading tongues. Great birds the size of emu and ostrich flutter in the sky, wings like insects, and hooves made of platinum. As distance grows between what land I knew and what universe I do not, I see great gods surrounding our world, orbiting the galaxy like planetary satellites, and know that these beings play both guardian and predator. Colossal creatures of invisibility and maddening impossibility that could erase Earth-bound existence in a single blink. Gods composed of plasma and stardust, sweeping tendrils and appendages that writhe and explore and search and stalk. In the places where faces should exist are only vapid darkness and at once I know what it is to understand a black hole.

And still, I float into emptiness. Still Earth shrinks to marble as I grow. Grow to a magnitude that belches laughter and widens eyes. Vomit excitement and fear into the cosmos that erupts as mineral and anti-matter, that births stars and devours planets. Clutch my aching stomach with arms that stretch into lightyears, and it is only in this rage-fuelled, dizzying euphoria that the beings of legend and myth fall away and in their absence I see it at last, hovering there in infinitum in this vast stretch of void-filled universe, a god of untamed power that has stretched the expanse of time and of which even I know that I will only ever witness a fraction of its whole.

The Great Eye...

...staring at me with unblinking wonder. Inside its gaze is the beginning and the end of time. Hidden in the eternal darkness of its pupils I watch as light erupts and matter breaks and planets form and oceans birth and cities rise and empires fail, and somewhere amongst it all I see the future as it was the past and as it will always be the present. Elder Gods and Great Old Ones slither along its lens, trapped like goldfish in a bowl, and as the Great Eye blinks my reality shatters and in my inner eye I see what may soon come to pass. A Red Queen's sigil, a burgeoning army of monsters and mutilations breaking across dimensions, the freeing of unnamable, uncountable gods that would snap their fingers and reduce our world to dust. I see Henry devoured by a mouth composed of teeth and tongue and boil, and a planet rubbed between monstrous fingers into rubble. I see my mother and father held captive in chains and tossed into the ether by great, unyielding hands, and a young girl, blonde dying under the rule of a Red Queen of Hearts.

The Great Eye opens.

The world falls away.

All sound is lost.

All sensation is memory.

All that was is Eye, and in the afterburn of its immense visage I see a book the size of continents. Pages that turn with sweeping gales and raging hurricanes. Opens to a page of wonderland. Pauses. Melts away.

And I am alone.

And I am shivering.

No...

Not alone.

I am with me. A reflection come manifest.

Standing in the black void, she approaches. The Other Alice. She is me, but she is not me. I am her, but I am not her.

She smiles.

I smile.

She blinks.

I blink.

She opens her mouth to speak.

Screams.

Dissolves.

Is lost.

Gravity rushes back with the blind anger of inherited vengeance, and I shatter.

Collapse.

Fall into darkness.

Laugh.

Cry.

Sleep.

Sleep...

Sleep.

Awaken to a silent world. A cold world. A ghoulish world of the dead.

Cautiously I rise, pushing against starved earth with hands now unblemished by cut or scrape or bruise. I examine my body for ailments, yet the only evidence I find of what came before are the tears and rips in fabric, and the scorch marks that hem my dress. It is small relief, however, my mind struggling to process the hallucinations and psychedelic marvels witnessed from the incredible fungi's power. I glance skyward, searching for the great and cosmic eye witnessed in my dream state and find only stars winking back at me. For the first time I wonder if we are truly alone, and if each blazing sun is or was ever once a titan floating in the ether. A shake of the head confirms that I do not desire answers. It is too much for such a fertile mind to comprehend.

Once calmed—as much as one can calm following the turning of an immeasurable illusory wheel—I direct my attention to this new chapter of my adventure. Long for sun-soaked beaches and radiant forests as skin prickles with chill and I take my first steps among the cracked graves and broken tombstones that speckle a graveyard stretching so far in each direction that I am left to wonder how I arrived here without my own knowledge and which path I am yet to take. For there is no clear path in either direction to see. Only unkempt patches of browned grasses and long-dead spectators. A low-lying fog covers the site like a blanket, and I am left with no option but to wander aimlessly ahead.

I walk with reverence among the buried corpses, absorbing the respite of event from this nonsense world. Though my skin shivers and my hairs stand to attention, I am grateful for this reprieve. I inhale long reams of cool mist, studying each grave that I pass as some internal compass gives me heading. I see names that I do not recognise, and some that I do, and I force myself to believe that what is written is not the truth of this world. That all that I have seen is not truth made reality. That all that I have tasted and smelled and touched and heard, is not all made truth.

Who can you trust when you cannot trust yourself?

"Wake up, Alice," I mutter to myself as my lip warbles yet my intent to complete this absurdist's mission is enflamed. "Wake up from this garish hellscape, please..."

Yet, whatever command I have over my quivering limbs and melting mind is dumb and blind and I continue onward, fighting to not flinch at each imagining of clatter and sound in the darkness, at each imagined shape that dances in the far-reaches of the mist, at each pebble that stabs my soles and makes me think of eyes and mouths and tongues and hands that claw at my ankle with intent to drag me on down into the gullet of trees.

We're all mad here.

I shake my head from the voice that is not mine yet is my own inside my head. "No. Mad people live in an asylum."

And where do you think you are right now?

I read the stones aloud, alarmed at the futility of my own voice. "Thomas Edlin, beloved father of Cynthia, Edward, and Rose. Husband to Patricia Edlin. Aged 45."

Poor, poor man.

"Winnifred Uxbridge. Gone, but never forgotten. Aged 94 years."

The worms feast upon us all in the end.

I speak louder, if only to drown this invasive dialogue

that accompanies each dictation. "Here lies the body of Ebeneezer Scrooge."

Ebeneezer? Even you must now know that madness has finally claimed you.

"No."

Fiction is not reality.

"Go away."

Go where? Where is left to run, Alice? How can you outrun yourself when you are bonded by blood and static and spit?

I clench my teeth and swallow dryly, doggedly pressing on. Try not to become overwhelmed at the volume of dead that lay here and the lack of the living. In this world I float like a specter among them, wondering what it is I look for and what form the key to escape may take. As I involuntarily increase my pace, I am thankful that the invasive voice has retreated, yet their words still ring inside my head like an echo hollered into the pits of despair.

We're all mad here.

And then I see it, looming out of the fog like a ship in the night. A sight which I have never seen but which I know I have been looking for since bestowed with my existence. A gravestone standing like a monument amongst its brethren. An altar, of sorts, proudly displaying its artistic fervour like the feathers of a peacock. Black and white marble is fashioned into shapes of strange deities and forgotten saviours, and it is as I approach the steps of the Dais that my heart pounds and the world holds its breath. My vision tunnels on the square block that stands central to the display, a stone box with a great eye carved onto its face. As I grip shaking fingertips to the lips of its lid, I feel the weight of my burden holding the object down, fighting to keep its secrets. With struggling arms and knotted muscles, I pull as the stone lid creaks protest and yields to the world. I shift the block enough to glance inside and find a bed of black velvet and white dust.

Nothing more.

Only the imprint of where a book may once have lain.

"You're too late, Alice."

I hear the voice that was inside my head speak outside my head and as I spin to face my guest I am met with expected absurdity. A great cat, bipedal and reminiscent of sphinxes and felines of Egyptian myth stands at the foot of the Dias. Her skin is black and furless, her head and clavicle crowned with jewels of purist gold. While her chest is bare, a fine skirt of unknown leather shrouds her waist, and as I drink in the majesty of this creature, I understand the face of my kin buried inside its facial features.

"Mother?"

She stares at me with a studious gaze, unflinching at the mention of our possible connection.

"You're a long way from home, Alice."

I nod. Know not what else to say.

"They have come. Beaten you to your goal. Taken that which you seek, and which shall put an end to all of madness." Her voice is silk, soothing to hear outside of my own mind.

"So, it's over?" I ask. "The Queen has won?"

She casts me a pitying gaze and I've never felt so young, so unwise to the world. "No."

"No?"

A long inhalation, an impatience to my naivety as she blinks and evaporates into a cloud of black smoke. When she speaks again, the voice is behind me, and I turn to find her sat coyly upon the stone ornament. "Those who have come are not those whom you should fear. Your enemies will soon arrive, of that there is no doubt. But for now, your secret is as safe as one can be when you hand an idiot the fragile glass of your existence."

"I do not understand. Who are they of whom you speak? What is your name?"

She grins, wide and terrifying as teeth bare and tail whips. "Are you mad, Alice?"

"Excuse me?"

"Are you mad?"

"No."

She laughs. I growl.

"Are you quite certain?"

I consider the question, already growing tired of riddles and wanting the answers I seek. "I am certain."

She turns up her lip. Nods. Blinks. Vanishes. Appears at my feet, curled around my ankles as a low purr rumbles in her stomach.

"What are you—"

Blink.

Smoke.

Appears behind me, hands clutching my shoulders. I gasp and pivot, meeting her nose only inches from mine. "It will not do you well to cling to sanity in Wonderland, Alice. Only in the lunacy of this land can you find true escape."

I reply through gritted teeth, force myself to forget my fish-father, crying an ocean of my own tears, the pursuit of the wasps, the burning of the nymph, and the vision of a blinking cosmos. "I'm not mad."

"That as may be," my cat-mother replies. "Though those you face next will test your resolve, of that I'm certain." She takes a step back and raises a thin arm to the distance. "Those who have claimed your prize reside in an eternal loop of endless infinitum. The rabbit has delivered unto them."

My ears prick up. "Rabbit—?"

My cat-mother continues, undeterred. "Soon you will wish you may return to this graveyard, where evidence lies around you that time is not immemorial, and consequence must follow all action. There is no meaning in the land where eternity survives."

"You mentioned a rabbit. What rabbit? Have you seen my brother?" I urge. Frown, take in the feline musk of her odour.

She grins. Cocks her head. Chuckles. And she is gone. Evaporated to smoke.

I am once more alone. Thoughts and wonderment of her words cycling through my mind as I wonder that my rabbit-brother has been here. That I am truly on track to progress. How long ago had he come? How much farther is he ahead? What is his purpose in this narrative unfolding beneath my dirt-caked feet?

In the absence of my cat-mother I stare longingly at the crypt of marble and find the lid has been replaced. Is now perfectly united with the stone, though I have no memory of returning it. The graveyard's silence pounds against my aching head and as my stomach protests and as I swallow desert, I turn in the direction she once pointed.

A light beckons in the distance, a breaking beacon among this place of decomposition.

Empty-handed, but with the witness of Henry's recent visitation renewing my resolve, I walk on and into the light...

CHAPTER 5
NECROTIC CELEBRATIONS

I stagger with tired legs until the all the graveyard's teeth rot, break, and crumble and all that is left is gum, cracked and parched like arid desert wastes.

The landscape is barren but for smatterings of springs of shrunken weed. Wind gusts pockets of dirty cloud and occasionally I am called to mask my eyes and mouth with my elbow crook. The sky hangs grey and thick, and I wonder if another storm will come soon. Though I see no lightning and hear no thunder, I detect something that crawls and swims among the duvet of clouds but remains ever hidden from its full reveal. At times I spot the shadow, silhouetted in the blanket. At other times a fin or leg, though at this juncture I question my own sanity and wonder that all that I knew of my mind is now gone.

Are you mad, Alice?

I walk until my legs grow weak and my feet grow sore. I walk until my throat shrieks for water, each dry swallow like the scratching of a thousand jagged beetles racing to my stomach. At first, the emptiness and reprieve from impossible creatures and hypnotic foliage was comforting, but now I long once more for ocean, I long for the beaches, I pray for forests and mushrooms and a break in the monotone to bring a palette of colour and wonder. Air with humidity. Jungle with calls of ape and song of bird. I am left with time to think in an infinite that is truly endless, and I see my rabbit-brother's ghost frolicking in the dust clouds, hear his fever dreams in my own addled mind, feel his skin on mine as though he is all around me and yet nowhere at all.

It is as I surrender hope and yield to my knees that the voices inside my head grow. They begin as giggles, double into chuckles, erupt into laughter, and taper into guffaws. Strange cackles from passerine throats, yet it is when I look up from the starved ground that I see them, wandering toward me as though they had always been a part of my world. As though my isolation was a yet another level of dream of its own creation.

They appear to me as hideous malformations of humans, goblinesque and torn from the pages of a children's book. Strange, elongated features mark the melted wax of their faces, hands draped to the ground, scoring the earth with knotted and gnarled fingers. Their chest cavities are as pronounced as tarp stretched along a network of tree branches, and their noses could puncture flesh. The wildest feature among the pair wasn't their bulb-like eyes or staggered steps, but the stretch of fleshy fabric that combined them together, holding their heads in place as though they were one.

The pair that is one hobble towards me, eyes fixed and unblinking. At first, I believe that they have no mouth or lips, until they are close enough to smell the briny stink of their odour and notice that what appeared to be a long scar that scratched from chin to ear was, in fact, a primitive mouth, jagged teeth like piranhas jutting across dry, lipless skin.

"Hello?" I ask, my voice a breath that is stolen by the wind.

They crane their heads to each other, revolving like broken doors. Their grins widen. They chuckle, the throttled choke of a petrol machine struggling to fire. With limping steps they pivot, one of the twins waving a ghoulish hand to beckon me forward. Before I can ask another question, they scurry at alarming speed, rooster tails of dust flaring in their wake.

I run, chasing after this new monstrosity. Though they have two pairs of hands and arms between them, they have somehow coordinated the efforts of their congealed bodies and each twin whirls their outer arm in a pendulum-like motion that brings to mind gorillas, chimps, and ape. They swing, feet curled to malnourished chest, and it is all I can do to keep to their slipstream. The ground, once barren, soon yields the first indication of ancient, broken buildings and determined plant-life. Cactuses stretch spindled fingers from the ground, rocks grow and swell like Russian dolls, and it is as I am breathless and wondering if my legs will carry me further that the collaborative creatures rent a blood-curdling screech and launch themselves impossibly into the trees that now surround me. One moment they are there, the next they are gone, as though they never were and never will be again.

I search the canopy for my guides, hunting among Jurassic leaves and Cretaceous fronds for signs of their existence. Somewhere above I fancy that I see the cat-like grin of my cat-mother. Teeth white against the browns and greens. Enlarged like a projected visage that should never be.

Where am I?

At some point in my feverish sprint, I found myself back in forest. I wonder if my wishes had turned true, the grotesque creature a kind of fairy guide for my wants and need, though the forest now surrounding me shares little of the brightness and fancy of my former environment. Here the trees are twisted and foreboding. Here they stretch across the sky as though caging me from daylight, casting the world in shadows and gloom. Here I am aware of an incessant buzz, and I fear that the waspish things have returned and that my race to freedom has yet to cease.

I hear voices.

Far off, yet somehow all around me the voices chatter and chant. They fade in and out as though someone scales and diminishes the volume of the record player, and as I am drawn forward, I find a break in the trees and see what becomes the most impossible sight of my journey thus far.

A long table.

A dozen dining chairs.

A hollow decorated as though for the celebration of a party that must have passed one hundred years prior. Balloons now black and brown that droop and wrinkle like broken egg sacs. Illegible banners, trembling in the wind like dried out shredded meat. Somewhere nearby, cracked and aged music plays through invisible speakers. A strange jig of saxophones, tubas, drums, and violin. A tune I've heard once before, a long time ago.

"Alice! So nice of you to join us." The voice comes from a man glimpsed through the distortions of a fun house mirror. His body is zigged and zagged, his eyes of different proportions. Atop his crown is a large top hat that may once have stood emerald green but which was now tattered and covered in grime. He beams. Motions a pale, waving hand. "Make room. Our esteemed guest has arrived at last."

"Beckoned by our festivities, no doubt," a second voice croaks. I'm startled to find a dishevelled hare sat beside the strange hatter, human-sized and twitching. His fur is matted and mottled, and wrapped around his breast by mere tatters of fabric is a grey waist jacket. "You can't deny the rhythm once the rhythm enters your soul."

"A musical tapeworm, if you will," the hatter announces.

"Indeed."

"Indeed."

My gaze settles on a third of their number, and in the seat flanking the hatter I spy my rabbit-brother, pale enough to be assumed a spirit. Atop his head his rabbit ears stand crooked, whiskers bent like lightning rods. His eyes are pale and rheumy, his gaze fixed on the cracked china cup nestled in the bosom of his hands, mirky tea sloshing dangerously as he shakes as though wrought with pneumonia.

"Henry?"

My rabbit-brother makes a startled utterance, eyes dashing to mine.

Returns to his tea.

The Hatter bellows a guffaw. "Please, Alice. Won't you join us? There's plenty to share."

"We've been waiting for an age," says the Hare.

For the first time I notice the strange array of items strewn along the length of the ancient table. To me it looks as though these creatures have been sat here since the dawn of time. Plates are buried beneath mounds of matter that was once food, but from which now grows bacteria and fungus and pops miniature clouds of spores around the hollow. Beetles and rats scuttle and mine the mounds, skirting the brittle edges of fine dining crockery now chipped, cracked, and defunct. Bones of former creatures stand like buildings in a toy city, and somewhere in the midst of it all a long tendril that might be a millipede, but which I strongly suspect is not, excavates and writhes.

I move towards the vacant seat beside my rabbit-brother. The chair feels unsteady in my hands, as though a press of the finger might collapse it to dust. To my surprise, it bears my weight.

"For you." The Hare tosses a loaded plate which lands with a loud crash before me. The china splinters to jigsaw pieces. Food slops in all directions. "Dig in, there's plenty to go around."

"Tea?" the Hatter asks, already pouring a waterfall of thick sludge from a large pot into a cup laden with holes. The gelatinous mess trickles on the table, stains his lap, but causes no discernible discomfort to his persons. With a swift throw, the cup smashes on top of my strange food pile. "Drink up, there's plenty to go around."

"Plenty to go around," the Hare echoes, taking a forkful of rotten meat. My stomach turns as he distends his maw wider than should be possible and chomps down on the fork. When he withdraws the utensil, only the handle remains.

I can still hear the chewing of metal on teeth when I turn to my rabbit-brother. "Henry? It is you, isn't it? Are you okay? Please, speak to me."

My rabbit-brother says nothing. Only shakes and stares vacantly.

"A quiet one, he is," the Hatter bellows. "Thought it might run in the family. You seem to have a lot of joy inside you. Volume. It's nice. We crave company. Sat here day after day, celebrating an end that never comes."

"The end," the Hare toasts through lips brimming with masticated offal.

"The end," the Hatter agrees. "We began to believe that this day would never come. The bringer of all that will break. It's wonderful, really. Makes it all seem worthwhile, after all."

I frown, gently sliding my chair away from the table as food crawls to its edge and trails to the forest floor. "What end? What are you celebrating?"

The Hare and the Hatter look at each other. On the table in front of them, the teapot rattles, something trapped inside hunting for escape.

"Freedom," they reply in sync. "Escape. Release."

"It's all we ever wanted," the Hatter says.

"It's all we ever desired," the Hare adds.

"It's all we ever needed," they say again in unison.

"Freedom from what?" I ask. "What are you escaping? Please, I need answers, no more riddles. What's wrong with my brother?"

The Hatter explodes with laughter. The Hare follows suit. Even my rabbit-brother cackles and chokes, hand to his mouth.

"So many questions," the Hare says.

The Hatter nods. Wipes black ichor from his running nose. "Here's a question for you: why is a raven like a writing desk?"

"Why is a... I'm sorry, what?"

The Hatter leers, leaning forward on his elbows. They sink into the sludge of plated food. "Why is a raven like a writing desk?"

I meet his eyes, cold and reptilian, for what feels like a

lifetime. Before I can offer any answer, both he and the Hare erupt into squawks of raucous guffaws, the sound like warring metal giants. Their mouths don't move, just hang open at an unnatural angle like twin horns sounding home sea-bound vessels, and as I clap my hands to my ears, pondering the last of the questions asked, the teapot in the centre of the table explodes into a thousand porcelain fragments. They shoot in all directions, a nail bomb dropped in the centre of us all, and although somehow I'm left unscathed, the shrieking has stopped, and I can at last remove my hands from either side of my head.

They're dead now—the Hare and the Hatter, at least. Blossoms of blood paint their clothes and flesh with crimson, their bodies folded as they take an eternal drink of the mush on their plates. The silence is unsettling, made only eerier by two things.

The first is my rabbit-brother, untouched, unchanged, unaware, staring vapidly ahead into space as though cast from wax. The only sign that he lives is the gentle wobble of his bottom lip, as though tomes of thoughts threaten to spill from an idle tongue with no mechanism to speak.

The second is the tiny creature settled in the place where the teapot had once been. Something that might once have been a mouse, but which now has been mutilated and transformed beyond all natural order. The size of a dinner plate, with too many appendages to count, each tentacle writhing and folding around each other like a pit of endless snakes. Tufts of fur, two mousy ears, and twitching whiskers take the middle of its mass, the only things that seem to make any sense.

For reasons unknown, even to myself, I reach across the grub-infested table and take a large spoon in shaking hands. Tentatively, I knock the writhing mass aside where it hits the forest floor with a dull, wet thud and crawls off with a strained squeak. I shudder, eyes drawn to the damp, stained cover of the book that had been hidden inside the teapot. The book swells in size, free of its bindings and, as it pulls itself open, reveals yellowed and cracked pages saturated with rough sketchings of creatures and monsters misunderstood, words written in an ancient script that I cannot decipher. I draw the tome closer to my chest and close the pages. Run a pale finger across the binding. Feel the tingle of static surge through my body.

Yes...

I have found it. This surely must be the item I have been seeking. The only quest I have ever known. In my hands... the Necronomicon.

Before I can explore its contents further, activity erupts around me. Stained against a sky, blood-curdled in the breaking of the clouds, dozens upon dozens of Nightgaunts disturb the air with membranous wings. Calls and shouts from ground-level accompany their assault, and as I whirl on the spot I can make out more figures approaching. Men and women in black robes decorated with crude red hearts.

My heart leaps. I clutch the Necronomicon tightly and flee this necrotic celebration, casting a longing look back at my rabbit-brother who appears unperturbed by the invasion. Somehow, deep down in the place where genetics remember better than living memory, I know that it is not truly him. I know that he will somehow survive. I know that they will protect his kind as he is one of them and they are one of him. Still, that doesn't stop the tears of sorrow streaming down my cheeks as my legs pump like pistons and I race into a weaving natural labyrinth of moss and leaf and bough. Snatches of vines whip my face, break my skin, scream tangled snatches of a phrase that will later haunt every nightmare that presents itself in sleep. "Why *is* a raven like a writing desk?"

And they're so close to me, now. Snatching at my heels. I imagine hounds comprised of black leather with teeth like bear traps and it's all I can do to keep running, book tucked beneath my arm. I have no destination in mind, only escape, and it's as I swerve around a trunk the size of houses and disturb a flock of neat, passerine black birds, that my mind idols and I think of ravens and desks and writing and—

—*home*—

—and Queens and monsters and fetid platters and—

—*Henry*—

—and Gaunts and fire and tombstones and feline grins and—

—tumble. Head over heels. Each flailing cartwheel is torture. Each collision with the ground is agony. My body is too young for this punishment as the world fades and I fall once more down rabbit holes and into colonies, the sound of the encroaching mob of winged and running creatures falling far behind, only their fading shouts for company.

It feels like eons before I finally reach my destination. For an indeterminate time that feels like no time at all, I lie there, battered and bruised. I tremble with exhaustion, mumble for mother, and it's only when the world that was blackness begins to glow in an underground cavern of mushrooms and glowing fungi that I begin to realise...

...I've gone nowhere much at all. The circle is complete. I have returned to a cavern I once filled with tears and transformed into an ocean. Run the girth of the world and returned to the start.

Only, instead of a waiting sea and a monster of mouths, carved into the bed of the rock face, there is now a door.

CHAPTER 6
THE MAZE THAT BLEEDS

Once, when I was a little younger than Henry is now, I witnessed something that I'd later come to know as a paradox.

I didn't know that that's what it was at the time. In my youthful ignorance I only knew that what I was viewing was both true and untrue, a fragmented reality of its own design. My grandfather, by then approaching eighty years of age, stood in the open doorway to the bathroom, the frail gossamer of his hair illuminated by the diluted streetlight filtering through frosted glass. He swayed slightly, finger to chin, debating some unknown purpose with himself.

"Papa?" I asked softly, afraid to startle him.

"Hmm?" He turned sharp, eyes lighting like beacons with fright, then dying to embers as his faculties settled within his aging mind. "Oh, Alice. You frightened me."

"Is everything okay?" I shuffled my feet on the hard-wood floors, gaze locked on his.

"Yes." He smiled and made jolly. "Everything is fine. I was just... just heading to bed." He lowered himself to his knees and took both my shoulders in a grasp far too firm for someone with hands as translucent as his. "You best do the same, dear. It's late."

For what felt like an infinity I stared into the sparkling pools of his eyes. While his body spoke of youth and awareness, his eyes held a secret that would later have Grandpapa bed-bound and spilling candle wax on his linens. It would be this secret that eventually announced itself and would see Papa wandering aimlessly into the next door's farm to live out his final moments trampled under the hooves of our neighbour's noble steed.

A paradox.

A secret lurking beneath the surface.

Truth, and untruth. He was fine, but he wasn't. He was here, but he was gone, flitting between two realities in the blink of an eye.

A paradox is what I now see. As I stare at the door, the walls that were once bare and unforgiving rock now glow in a strange chirography of rune and script that are both there and not there. Truth and lies. Present and imagined. Images that had lain dormant awaken and speak to me, whispering in languages I can't understand, but which set my senses aflame. Sharp, undeniable, geometric edges, impossible in the rock, like luminous veins of blood brought forth by an invisible artist's hand. I marvel at their work, attempt to translate their meanings, and yet somehow know it all at once. I have awoken them. It has begun. With the small, tattered book that becomes the key beneath my arm I have released them and activated their power. A book of wondrous things and unknown potential, held in the hands of an innocent, naive girl.

I clutch the book before me. Open to the first page and stroke the leaf. Ink, long dried, paints the page from eons before, untranslatable and alien. Markings and pictographs reflect some of the same decoration etched on the cavern walls, and as I file through each page in turn, I find my eyes grown wider, my breath come in small hitches. A static fills the air and I don't know whether to laugh or cry.

Footsteps echo behind me.

I gasp. Snap the book shut. Reach for the door's handle and find none. With a gentle nudge of my tender shoulder it yields, as if waiting for me all these long years. I charge ahead, emerge through its portal, find the door has already closed behind me before I can address my personal security. In front of me the cavern opens, yields a fantasy realm, and here I stand above all things.

An impossible kingdom sprawls ahead of me, an ancient oil painting come manifest. Ribbons of autumnal reds stain hedges that knit together in a labyrinth that could give Daedalus cause for envy. Buds of white blossoms scar the brush like acne, and above it all, heaven bound and oppressive, a swirling spiral of clouds roil and bubble. The dark shapes witnessed in a distant graveyard have returned to the skies, always present, never quite revealed, dragons and cephalopods and primal monsters of myth adrift in an ocean of gas and cloud that stretches into the ether.

Standing at the labyrinth's end...

...a castle.

The castle stands proud and foreboding, each brick coloured, designed and shaped as if to cause the onlooker physical alarm and pain. In the way that nature paints its dangers in reds and golds, this construction pulses with a crimson magnetism that dissuades my progress. I know I must go onward, though I fear what may happen if I do. Dark windows stare at me like empty eye sockets, the crenelations of each parapet and balustrade like jagged teeth on an open maw.

I know they are inside.

I fear that they are inside.

Oh, God. I must go inside.

I look down at feet, find a thin staircase built into meadow that descends into the gates of the labyrinth. It is the only path, one designed to guide forward and offer no simple escape. Each step I take encourages knocking knees, and it is only as I reach the final step—or what I believe to be the final step—that I realise my error in assumption. What I had thought to be the blood-red carpet of the labyrinth is in fact the ceiling of the liquid that lies beneath. Waves and ripples cast by an unseen gust disturb the water, and I only pause a moment before I continue my descent. Submerge my ankle, then my calf, the lily white of my flesh stained pink. The water is warm, fanning my pinafore around me like a ballgown. My hips submerge. My chest. My shoulders. I do not bother to hold my breath for I know that these waters are not that of the land of the living and in dreams and nightmares I may breathe and live and survive. One more step takes me under, and though each individual strand of blonde hair floats and ululates in the gentle current of this tepid red sea, I find my assumptions confirmed. I find breath, and I am okay. Though, I understand that I am a fool, and what I believed to have been a monstrous land above the surface is nothing to what this monolithic underwater dimension presents. Though my gravity is held sturdy below me by a nest of vine and pondweed, I can see into the monstrous depths to the places where light is swallowed by the hungry darkness and dead things live. Dark, mutilated shapes skim in shoals, chased by predators and lost to the blinking horizon in a matter of moments. Flowers and coral decorate patches where rock has attempted to drink sunlight, a thousand colours and formations of breeds unknown to man and that will never be fully revealed to surviving history.

I find no other option but to journey into this maze.

I tread carefully to begin with, the rational side of my mind screaming the implausibility that I find myself inside. Decisions are made for me, the decrepit book of secrets untouched by its own protective bubble, whispering lefts and rights and onwards until I am well and truly lost in the labyrinth's depths. I fight to keep my gaze pointed, knowing that no good can come from examining the growing mass of swimming creatures circling beneath the tangled vine carpet. I breathe without bubbles and air, each step grown in confidence as I begin to wonder if I could swim or float to sustain my progress. A brief attempt at a hop turns fruitless, gravity resumed normal to a life above sea level, and I tread onwards, all too aware that soon a castle will greet me, and in its clutches I must burden myself with a final decision.

Right.

Right.

Forward.

Left.

Right.

Forward.

Left.

Right.

"Alice?"

I pause, snapped out of my hypnotic revery by the familiarity of the voice. Turning about in all directions to identify the speaker, I find myself painfully alone.

Step.

Step.

"Alice."

Firmer now, a rasp to accompany a voice of pain and struggle. It is only when I look to the bleeding aquatic hedgerow that surrounds me that I notice a break in the repetitive patterns of leaves and branches. A face protrudes, sick and rosy, eyes white and without pupils.

"Father?"

My fish-father has become an unshapely atrocity. His form now moulded into the bush, he appears more as a barnacle or fungus than the strange sea creature of before. Where legs and arms should have been are only roots and tangles, and I note with pained anguish that the rise and fall of his chest is laboured and forced.

My fish-father offers a weak grin, a scab breaking open to spit its pus. "You found it."

He glances to the book, his smile breaking wider. The effort of it causes his face to shrivel and wrinkle. For a moment, the whites of his eyes fade to grey.

"I did," I reply. "I can free you. I can free us all."

He nods, painfully slow. "Ph'nglui mglw'nafh Cthulhu R'lyeh wgah'nagl fhtagn."

Something flickers behind his vapid gaze, and for the first time since entering his company I wonder at the rippling knot in my stomach. I had heard this chant before, a strange language unbeknownst to myself. Black robes and red hearts.

"What does that mean?" I ask.

My fish-father smiles, eyes grown drowsy. "It is the enchantment needed to break the spell. The dialogue of the Elders and the Great Old Ones. Study it, Alice. Learn it well."

"Say it again. Slowly." Though I beg for the repeat, I already understand its message. Hear its translation in whispers inside my head. The book shudders in my clutches.

"Ph'nglui mglw'nafh Cthulhu R'lyeh wgah'nagl fhtagn."

In his house at R'lyeh, dead Cthulhu waits dreaming.

My gaze drifts to the depths beneath me. For the first time I can see punctuations of architecture at its farthest reaches. Great blocks of masonry unknown to this world, shining in emerald and opal. Nearby, a great column rises to join the location I imagine the castle to sit, forming the great stone pillar of its foundation. A single thread to connect this waking world to the lost and sleeping city in the depths.

Below, great bubbles rise, as if released from the organs of a slumbering giant.

Ph'nglui mglw'nafh Cthulhu R'lyeh wgah'nagl fhtagn.

"You must onward, Alice," my fish-father says. "Time is short. The end is nigh."

He cranes his neck forward, as if momentarily forgetting his lack of limbs. I give a small nod, then turn away without word. My senses are ignited, and I fear that I have gained new information that shatters the perspective acquired from this illusion of reality. My foundations of knowledge stand as frail as the knitted carpet beneath my tender feet as I pursue the end, take left, take right, move onward, wholly aware that beneath the impressive construction of this architectural peak that can only truly be the summit of the fabled R'lyeh, dead Cthulhu waits dreaming.

"Henry..." I mutter, alarmed by the weakness of my own voice. "Hold on just a little longer. I'm coming."

Forward.

Right.

Right.

Left.

Step.

And there the great door stands proud. There the titanic entrance to the castle beckons me forward and repels me in equal measure. There, above the obsidian doors that stand as tall as giants, a beating heart throbs and bleeds its ichor into the crimson ocean, each droplet a spurt of ink that forms a mirky cloud and fades.

When did the castle submerge beneath the waters?

There, somewhere deep in the chasm of myth and legend, fable and imagination, I know that She awaits.

The Red Queen.

Ph'nglui mglw'nafh Cthulhu R'lyeh wgah'nagl fhtagn.

I can almost hear the chanting mob awaiting. I can almost see Her grin. Above the heart, a shape forms, a bipedal feline with a grin as wide as her wingspan. She grins down upon me and purrs.

I am confirmed.

The time is nigh.

Metal shrieks on metal. A great lock clicks. The castle doors open wide to greet me.

At the threshold the creature awaits. My cavern pursuer. All limbs and eyes and gelatinous flesh. A slave to their will. The great obedient monstrosity built for a single purpose by the Elder Things.

I close my eyes, feel the enveloping wrap of its slime-ridden, oozing embrace, and I am carried, absorbed into its flesh, its body made conduit.

There I am carried into the reception halls of the great R'lyeh.

CHAPTER 7

A COSMIC QUEEN

O nce I was not form, but mere matter, a shapeless creation awaiting consciousness. In the miasma of my maternal cocoon I was moulded, limbs given length, face awarded features, senses awakened from the cosmic gelatine of my mother's womb.

In sleep I dreamed. Of the external world I knew little, yet also I knew all. The delicate buds of blossoming ears digested warped and muffled sounds, the deep baritones of my father, the sweet tenor of my mother, the call and rush of society and life. With unseeing eyes, I drew a picture of a world far from that I would come to know, and in my pre-natal darkness I witnessed stars forming shapes of origins and wonder.

I see them all now.

Through the membranous translucency of the monstrosity's jelly, colours and shapes twist and break like light through a kaleidoscope. Muffled sounds collide and warp into a din that is both muted and absolute. I see imaginings of shapes that might be the robed cult of hearts but could just as well be pillars of stone architecture or the presence of more of this creature's kin.

I am not afraid.

In this maternal case I am rocked steadily into a light trance. The monstrosity's progress is smooth, its inner workings warm and soothing. Organs swim and squirm around me, sentient in their own design, and on occasion I am want to laugh and smile with them. Dance their frivolous dance as though one with my captor.

I hold the book. My totem of sanity. The key to my prison.

It is almost time.

I feel it in every fibre. It screams along passages of marrow in my bones. It ignites each nerve and swarms me with ecstatic fervour.

I see his face.

Not the fake Henry. Not the mutilated misrepresented form of my rabbit-brother that this world has produced, but my real brother. The one I know to be true. I see his face in the folds of jelly, smell his odour through nostrils choked with slime, hear his laughter as though he is everywhere and nowhere all at once.

Soon we will all be free.

Ph'nglui mglw'nafh Cthulhu R'lyeh wgah'nagl fhtagn.

In his house at R'lyeh, dead Cthulhu waits dreaming.

And then I am expelled.

The monstrosity spits me upon the underwater rug in one sharp expulsion of saliva and drool. I roll over. Unspool my body. Rise to my feet. She is waiting, the Red Queen. Sat upon an obsidian throne of coral barbed with thorns, she leers down upon me, an ungodly creature of creation. Once human, perhaps, she is one of the few creations in this wonderland to bear no resemblance to family or familiars. Robes clothe her frame in deep slashes of burgundy and crimson, a white ruff encircling a neck of flesh so pallid and waxy that I wonder how her corpse has not bloated beneath this ocean. Eyes of matching black to her throne glint with cold unkindness, and upon her right cheek throbs the malignant, swollen organ of a beating heart, cancerous and haunting. Black specs swarm the undulating mass, and it is upon closer inspection that I understand the forms of small black fish and crawling tardigrades that feast upon the black ichor spilling in steady billows with each rhythmic beat.

I hold the book in clasped hands behind my back as she leans forward with intense intrigue. Around me I am aware of the waiting audience, a hundred robed members of her zealous cult in a preacher's hall. They hum beneath their breath, a steady whisper of words now known and mistrusted in my mind.

"Ph'nglui mglw'nafh Cthulhu R'lyeh wgah'nagl fhtagn."

"You are she?" the Red Queen asks, her voice the screech of nails on chalkboard. "The girl expected?"

"So, I am told."

"And you have brought the item with you?" I know she knows, though the game must be played.

I remain silent.

"Show me," she commands.

"You first," I answer, knowing deep in the hollow of my malnourished stomach that her secret is greater than mine.

At first, she appears taken aback, her demeanour faltered. When the smile returns to her face, she grins wide. Parts lips that may just be scars on her face and reveals gums topped with teeth like shattered glass shards. "You are more than you appear, Alice."

"As are you." I raise my chin. Picture Henry. "Show your true self. The one that demands obedience from your subjects and has haunted the steps of my journey to this place."

The Red Queen gives a placating nod, and as she closes her eyes her form begins to shift and swim. Breaking apart in a thousand places, what had been the solid material of her matter becomes threads of genetic creation. Dark shapes swarm in a black mass of electric eels, writhing, bucking, wrestling with reality. As I try to track single beings, I find myself dizzying, and it's only when I blink that she stops, and I see what I have guessed to be true.

On the throne sits my fish-father.

"Hello, Alice."

Before I can offer retort, she's shifting again. Her transformations are rapid, frequency increasing with each passing second. One moment she is my fish-father, the next a flaming canine-nymph of terrible assembly. In the next a Gaunt of night, swiftly superseded by the visage of my cat-mother. With a wave of nausea, she is the malformed goblin twins, the Hatter, the Hare, and soon she is my rabbit-brother. In the next instant she has returned to my cat-mother, shifting between each form with an unrivalled fluidity designed to unsteady a mind already fragile enough to be treading the sword's edge.

"Is this what you wanted, Alice?" her voice calls, a polyphonic echo of tones and pitches. "Have I satisfied your curiosities now? Are your suspicions of the truth confirmed enough that you will now take your final steps and complete what has been written in the stars for eons past?"

Hot tears sting my eyes, the water projecting gusts of unseen waves that knock me unsteady with each shift of her form. I brace myself as the rising tide of cultish chanting steadily rises, and before I know it, I am shouting, calling with the passion of the gods of Olympus to know her true form. "Show yourself!" I command. "Shed this falsity and reveal what is true."

Laughter erupts around me, and for a moment I glance in all directions expecting to see her in swarms. Instead, I spy illusions of cat-like grins hovering like encircling birds, no body or master fixed to their leer.

"Show yourself!"

The laughter fades and the mouths disappear. I turn my gaze upon the throne and fear that it is all finally over. My mind now broken. Shattered. Madness consumed. For, sitting boldly upon the onyx coral throne, is a creature of alien design. One would be foolish to describe it as humanoid, though some features recall the gait and appearance of man. A tripod of insectoid legs holds the figure steady on the ground, spindly, yet with flesh that appears both soft and hard at once. A torso both thin and muscular stretches from the waist towards shoulders where two skeletal arms trail toward the ground. At their end are bony appendages. Four skeletal fingers capped with scythe-like claws that appear as though they could pierce the very fabric of reality. Yet, even with all this detail, it is not the body of this impossibility that alarms me the most. For, sitting upon the stretch of skin where shoulders should be but is only neck, is a vapid black hole rimmed with teeth and canvassed with melting flesh from which swarms a mane of squirming appendages. I am reminded of worms and stick insects and cuttlefish all at once, and I can fight the acidic tide no longer as vomit rises to my lips and spills into the crimson sea. In front of me it floats as a sand-coloured cloud, temporarily blocking her visage, though the relief is short lived as, without evidence of a working vocal cord, the mouth announces, "You know what it is that I am."

And I do. At first, as I arrived on the golden shores of this land I did not, but in the possession of the pages of this ungodly book I hold, and in the memory of my encounter with my fish-father within the labyrinth who was not my fish-father from the verdant shores, I understand her trickery. She is Nyarlathotep. The 'Crawling Chaos.' A creation of mischief, manipulation and devilry that would set even the great Norse Loki to shame. One that would trample upon Eris, Wisakedjak, and the Monkey King to throw their deeds into the footnotes of an archaic history.

A cosmic myth made manifest before me. Revealed in wonder, alarm, and terror. In the thrum of the power of the book clasped in juvenile hands I see her history with no beginning and no end, her travel and journey through space and time. She is the lynchpin of this world, the imaginer of this hallucinogenic reality, and it is to her that every whim and wonder and molecule of this world is served.

"The book, girl," Nyarlathotep croons. "It is time. Make good what is mine."

"You shall not awaken him," I reply, hands trembling under the power of her presence. "I know what it is you seek, and I will not allow it to pass."

"And what is it you believe to be true?" She is playing with me. Curious and entertained at my boldness.

"You are confined. A vessel trapped in a reality of your own design," I say. "I do not know how this has come to pass, but I know that you must awaken the others of your ilk to destroy the doorway to my dimension. Cthulhu is the first domino. Awaken the Great Old Ones and perhaps the Elder Things will follow. Your kin. Drawn to the flurry of your escape they will swarm my world and break it. Return modernity to the primordial. It is this chaos that you seek."

Nyarlathotep sits forward, rests spindly elbows on knobbly knees. "Very good, child. You know much. Then you will also know what you must do. What is destined to pass."

I take a breath to steel myself. Nod. Bring the book from behind me. In an instant I feel its pull as though magnetised toward this ancient cosmic being. I grasp it tightly, white knuckles shaking, yet it tugs with untold urgency.

"Why me?" I ask, wrestling that which should be inanimate. "That's what I fail to understand. Why am I chosen?"

"Why is anyone chosen?" the Crawling Chaos returns, appendages writhing and undulating in invisible currents. "Why does anything occur? What is the purpose of presence? What is the intent of creation other than to be and to not? For eons your kind has sought answers, begged for purpose, cried for reason, killed for order, and isn't it in this quest for sanity that insanity is allowed to thrive?"

The book slips. An inch. I tighten my grip. Fingers throb. A page threatens to tear.

"Release it, Alice." She is bored with me. It is inevitable. "You have no power here. Your part is played."

"Then why not take the book yourself?" I ask. The book slips further. The cult of hearts watches beneath the shadows of their hoods, chants grown louder. "If the power of the Necronomicon is all you need to unlock the door and break this reality, why leave it in the hands of a young girl?"

The first sign of fear ripples across her body. She shakes it away, attempts composure. "Too many questions."

"You know what I think? I think you fear me. I think there is something within my power that you are terrified of. Something that you cannot control. You say that my part is played, yet here we are. Because you are not the master puppeteer in this performance, are you? There is a rebel in your midst. An Outer God that you do not control." I think of my fish-father, of his words cast upon the shores of a tropical beach oh so long ago. One of their kind without a modicum of malice. The vessel that found me first. "There is still one being that you fear."

The great vapid hole of Nyarlathotep's maw shudders and snaps. From the depths of its abyss rise a dozen tendrils, the purple of day-old bruising, slugs stretched and pulled like liquid caramel, and in a sudden surge they snake toward the book that wriggles in my grasp. A single word reports from all directions, fills my head, pierces drum and canal, enough to make me want to release the book and clap my hands to my ears—

—"*Enough!*"—

—and yet in this moment I muster strength enough and draw the book toward my bosom. Fight bleeding ears and trickling nostrils. Before the snaking monstrosities can reach me, I throw the Necronomicon's pages open and find what I know to be there. What has been whispered and feared in the tumultuous air since my first descent into this madness. In the centerfold of the ancient pages, a great blazing eye stares at me. Unblinking. Omnipotent. Everything. I utter words that were never learned, speak in tongues of the Elders, and just as the tendrils slime and slicken the ancient pages my head is rocked back, my eyes rolled into infinite, and I am gone from this world.

A stark serenity washes its calms over each cell. I am all, and I am nothing as I float in this expanse of endless cosmic wonder. There is no direction, no up, no down, only unknowable volumes of glittering stars amongst beds of purple and crimson nebula. Galaxies eddy like weeds in the bay, universes spiralling in twisted and infinite patterns and constellations. I need not breathe. I need not blink. I need not taste or hunger or worry or thirst or love or delight or exist. We are one and one is we and somewhere in the never-ending canvas of a universe that eclipses my Earth-bound life I see a disturbance. A scar fractures across the whole, slits like blade to flesh, bleeds a great and wondrous eye that awakens and blinks its terror into the cosmos. I am but a child, staring up at an impossible moving portrait, and in the fiery torrents of its gaze I am broken, and yet I am healed. This being of no age and of no real destination and of no creator breaks upon me like waves to rock and I am humbled in its presence.

I know this creature. I have seen it before. A mushroom leading the journey that glimpsed me into madness.

Azathoth. That is its name.

And I am finally surrendered mad.

Azathoth stares at each fragmented part of my floating creation. Its stare reaches me in the threshold before its lids and in the vast distance of galactic matter that unites all that once was and will never be again. I speak with words that come not from lips but from intention and this wondrous magic of the unspoken dimension, and a flicker of the slitted, lizard pupil gives me confirmation as the great Azathoth blinks and closes and resumes its darkness in a powerful maelstrom of energy. Black holes blossom, devour planets. Stars that were once great now sputter and slip into shadow. Meteors and comets halt their paths. My tormented body gathers and folds and in the slip of the suction of this great cosmic sinkhole I find myself falling through time, falling through expanse, falling through space, falling...

...falling...

...falling...

...falling down the rabbit hole...

...falling through the ocean...

...falling across the forest floor...

...falling through broken stones...

...falling through tables of bonemeal and corpses...

...falling through bloodied labyrinths...

...falling...

...falling...

...I gasp.

Eyes snap open. Nyarlathotep beams with maw agape, tendrils retreated. I hear rumblings and there is both confusion and fear and joy sketched into her being. The cult whispers in words of wonder and terror, and I am aware that the castle is shaking. The foundations are trembling. Something terrible is awakening, and in this moment I wonder if I am too late. If the deed is truly done and the lunatics have left the asylum.

The chants grow ever louder as the wall to my right crumbles and drifts into the crimson sea.

"Ph'nglui mglw'nafh Cthulhu R'lyeh wgah'nagl fhtagn."

"Ph'nglui mglw'nafh Cthulhu R'lyeh wgah'nagl fhtagn."

"*Ph'nglui mglw'nafh Cthulhu R'lyeh wgah'nagl fhtagn!*"

Great torrents of bubbles rise and what I believed to be seabed and corral-strewn floor is now moving and shifting as a great titan rises to its full stature.

"Ph'nglui mglw'nafh Cthulhu R'lyeh wgah'nagl fhtagn!"

I am held in desperate fascination at the behemoth that breaks the ocean's surface and swallows the sky. The monster that swells and spreads. The great Elder God that is Cthulhu. Not of dragon, not of man, not of cephalopod, but a mutilation of all three. A monstrous god awakened with eyes blazing furious with rage. Clouds gather above, thunder and lightning roiling in the blackening cotton as rain pelts in sheets and soaks this world, commanded by his mighty presence. The cult claps and jeers, chants and quakes, and with one titanic swipe of his claw the roof of the castle is destroyed and the rippling fabric of space opens a portal to a familiar dimension. Above me, through the warbling mirror, I see my house, my garden, my forest, my world, and as tears blur my eyes, I hear the Crawling Chaos erupting in triumph.

"Yes! The time has come, my friends. Arise! Awaken! Claim what is your birth right. Escape this tormenting prison."

I step to the creature, book shut tight in one hand. Wonder if her tendrils beat me to my magic as she opened the portal and awakened the gatekeeper. Wonder that my visit to the great cosmic everything was a mere dream and nothing more. Wonder that there is any hope left and that all that I once knew was now gone, folded closed within the pages of this book.

She senses my proximity. Splutters a cry that might be a choke, and before the tendrils may surface, I plunge the book into the bowels of her vapid throat. Teeth clamp around my wrist and as I wrestle free a few drops of blood find her tongue.

But it is done.

The book cuts her airways. Restricts existence. Glows

with bioluminescent wonder as its matter melds with her flesh.

She staggers. Falls. Writhes in blissful agony on the ground.

Behind her, the great Cthulhu unleashes a roar into the thunderstorm, calls to its kin. Creatures of monstrous magnitude fall from the sky, crash into the ocean, send oncoming tsunamis to wash upon the zealous cult with no gratitude for their service.

Yet, somehow, even amidst this chaos, I smile as I crane my neck to the sky.

Settled on the crumbling rim of the broken castle roof is a small figure. Rabbit-like, and brother-like, and full of comfort. Beside him sits my fish-father—his true form, and not some twisted labyrinthine pet. Beyond them both, in the place where the portal has rented, blinks a great and monstrous eye, all-encompassing and wreathed in flame. I laugh, the sound as alien as all of this world has been and ever will be. I blink, and in the time it takes for the snap of darkness to take me, great waves thrash in pulsing torrents, threaten to destroy my body. But it is okay. Cosmic tentacles and tendrils have captured me. Wrapped me in their womb. I am taken into the bosom of Azathoth, pulled into the closing portal that snaps closed like a blinking eye. Its touch is maternal. Its power is whole. And as my flesh ripples through dimensions and I break this cosmic boundary, I release a great sigh. Darkness claims me, and all that I know is starlight.

I am uncertain if I am awoken first by sunlight, or by the summoning of my name.

"Alice?"

I stir, pain lighting like fire across my body. I taste dust and wood and find my body laid on hard ground.

"Alice? Are you okay?" My brother's voice. Innocent, inquisitive. "Are you dreaming?"

I pull my eyes apart, lids splitting like breaking scabs. I cough dust from my mouth and right myself. I am on my brother's bedroom floor, light flooding through gaps in the curtains, motes of dust waltzing majestically in the disturbance of my breath. My head pounds, and as I raise a hand to my brow my mind fills with visions of oceans and castles and monsters and queens, and I am upright, alert and terrified as I hunt this small space for the tell-tale signs of their existence.

"Alice? What is it?" Henry sits forward, sheets pooled around his waist. "You're scaring me."

They are gone. Vanished. There is nothing here that may signal reality to my imagination. I take a long breath and meet my brother's gaze, noting that some of the colour has returned to his cheeks. His eyes are bright, keen, and I wonder how long I have been lost in slumber. "Henry?"

"Yes, silly. Who did you think it was?" He chuckles, the sound like cleansing water to a wound. "Were you having a bad dream?"

"Yes..." I frown, struggling to process. "I suppose you could say that." I peel back the curtain, examine the garden. A small brown rabbit nibbles the grass. Normal. Usual. Ordinary. "It all felt so real."

And it did. I take a moment in this new silence and process my descent into madness. The great fighting forces of cosmic wonders manipulating their escape, fighting for freedom. A Dreamworld, adjacent to this one and yet a thousand leagues apart, filled with monsters that should never be. I had imprisoned them. Stalled their efforts. Thwarted their attempts of escape. Barred them in the final moments of a forthcoming triumph. Witnessed realities that should never have been.

Or had I imagined it all? With every passing second the sludge of sleep fades. Dreams that had been so vivid as to be recognised as reality blurring, and I am left scratching and searching for each detail.

A dream.

That's all it had been.

A nightmarish dream.

"Alice?"

"Yes?"

"Can we go outside, today? I miss the warmth of the sunshine."

I offer what I hope to be an encouraging smile. "Of course. I'll fetch Mother and Father first. Tell them that you're feeling better." I stroke his soft cheek, feel the bones beneath his thin flesh. "They'll want to give you your medicine still, okay?"

"Okay."

I smile. Cup his cheek. "I love you, brother."

"I love you, too."

I pause with my hand on the door, stare about the room. A gnawing sensation tickles the back of my head and my gaze fixes on the cover of the book on his nightstand. No longer decorated with an illustrated dragon creature, but instead with a clean, red heart upon its face.

I falter. See the concern on my brother's face. Offer him a reassuring smile. Thank my stars that the ghoulish nightmare has ended and exit the room with a fresh gait of excitement at the dawn of a new day.

Blissfully unaware that, through the closed door of the room behind me, my brother sits unblinking, gaze set at the farthest wall.

Blissfully unaware of the creeping things snaking their way up his airways.

Blissfully unaware of the sardonic grin that stains lips now licked with the steady sway of purple tentacles.

Blissfully unaware that, despite all my efforts, She has come.

And She is hungry for chaos.

AUTHOR'S NOTES

Call me crazy (and there are many that do), but I find more logic in the illogical and the inexplainable than I do in so-called "reality."

It's a wondrous thing, falling down the rabbit hole. Finding yourself opening up parts of your brain to ideas and concepts that can never be proven—and can never be *dis*proven. I think that's why I love Alice so much. Take a young, innocent girl and throw her into a land of wonder and impossibilities, and you have a formula for a timeless classic. At least, that's what Lewis Carroll thought in his original adventures when he created the lunacy that has transcended time and lives in all of our hearts no matter your age. I still remember the first time watching the Disney adaptation of "Alice's Adventures in Wonderland," lying on my family's living room carpet staring up at the TV. Everything was so colourful. Everything was so lustrous. Everything was so...

...insane.

I forgot about Alice for some time. In my teenage years, the idea of Alice's Adventures never once crossed my mind as I attended to my own adventures and found wonderland in friends and in the bottom of a bottle (before you say anything, I was at university, and drinking was never a true problem for me... kinda). It was only when the Tim Burton adaptation emerged on our screens that I re-discovered Alice, as well as the Mad Hatter, and the lunacy of the Bandersnatch and Jabberwocky.

It's all fiction. That's what I believed at the time. Fantastical fiction spawned from the mind of a distant writer with an imagination fertile enough to rival the best of our fantasy creators today.

And then I discovered the work of H.P. Lovecraft.

Now, you can call me cynical, or you can call me an existentialist, but the truth is that I've never truly believed in "Gods" as most religions know them. I've always had a wondering if there is something larger out there, and if the ego of humanity had so swelled within itself as we developed that we all forgot that maybe we're not the apex.

This is how I interpret Lovecraft's work. A scientific brain that thinks outside of the realm of science. A visionary (albeit a problematic one, but that's by-the-by) who understood the concept that maybe in the same way ants are to our boot, we are minuscule and insignificant to unseen forces. The cosmos is infinite, and we are less than a grain of sand.

I think this is why I'm drawn to Lovecraftian ideas. In a world where there is no sense, we embrace that there is no sense to be found. We explore the helplessness of knowing that at any point we may be snuffed out of existence, rubbed between two titanic fingers and crumbled to dust.

And so, it only felt right that I could have some fun exploring the combination of these two concepts. Of taking the wonder and the bizarro of Carroll's "Alice" and limning the tale with the cosmic hypnotism of the "Cthulhu Mythos." Long-time readers of mine will notice the tone and style of this story differentiates from my usual as I tried to capture the tone and feeling of a true Lovecraftian piece. It was tough, but boy was it fun.

I know I'm not the first to embrace this challenge of combination. In researching for this book, I came across a number of multimedia works that have scratched the same itch as I have explored in this book. This is but my adaptation and my expression of two master works that have, and will continue to, transcend time and space as it permeates through our cyclical canon and lexicon. I hope you liked reading it as much as I enjoyed writing it.

Of course, I can't close out this book without a special thanks to a select few who helped this book come to fruition. A massive thank you to the team at Hawk & Cleaver's "The Other Stories" who allowed me to pitch this idea and produce the audio version of this tale for our 2023 Halloween special. If you loved reading the book, you can find a *free* audio adaptation on our podcast, available on all podcast apps—go, now!

A huge thank you to all the horror readers that continue to support my work, including those that read the advanced copy of this story to provide feedback (thanks to Billie, Pam, Pat, Barbara, Cat B., Emily, and Mayra).

Another thanks to all the horror writers that continue to inspire my work and support my journey. This year has been a big one in finding a community of incredible talent who continue to drive my ambition and challenge what I'm capable of. Among those who have had a huge impact this year are Gemma Amor, Luke Kondor, Neil McRobert, Ally Wilkes, Sam Rebelain, Andy Boyle, Aaron Dries, John Crinan, to name a few.

A quick shoutout to the one who motivated this journey, and the one that still sits at the centre of my heart in all that I do and create. Bailey, know that I wouldn't have achieved any of this writing success without you in my life. Daddy loves you.

One final thank you goes to the endless and invaluable support provided by my personal jet pack strapped to my back throughout this wondrous journey we call life. Thank you, Sam, for everything you have done, and everything you continue to do. I didn't realise just how much I needed my own personal cheerleader until you continuously jumped and celebrated by my side (you must be exhausted by now).

And that's quite enough indulgence from me. Thank you, dear reader, for making it to the end of this book. No writer has a career without your generous time and dedication to reading the pages of these books. Know that you do amazing work, and you are seen.

Thank you...

...to Azathoth and back.

Daniel Willcocks

Sept 26th 2023

CLAIM YOUR FREE HORROR STORIES

Check out Dan's "Free Library" and join thousands of horror fans already benefitting from monthly free stories, exclusive discounts, BTS updates, and more.

Oh, and please consider leaving a review for this book.

LISTEN TO THE AUDIO

Dive into "The Other Stories'" 7-part audio journey, based on this book!

A fully produced audio tale, with full cast, audio production, narration, and SFX.

Bring the tale of Alice alive by downloading for **FREE** on your favourite podcast app.

ABOUT THE AUTHOR

Daniel Willcocks is an international bestselling author and award-winning podcaster of dark fiction. He is one quarter of digital story studio, Hawk & Cleaver; co-founder of iTunes-busting fiction podcast, 'The Other Stories;' CEO of horror imprint, Devil's Rock Publishing, author coach and founder of Activated Authors; ; and the host of the 'Activated Authors' podcast.

Residing in the UK, Dan's work explores the catastrophic and the strange. His stories span the genres of horror, post-apocalyptia, and sci-fi, and his work has seen him collaborating with some of the biggest names in the independent publishing community.

Find out more at www.danielwillcocks.com

facebook.com/willcocksauthor

twitter.com/willcocksauthor

instagram.com/willcocksauthor